Another Wildside paperback original, continuing this new series collecting the early pioneering pulp magazine novelettes of John Russell Fearn, presenting the first-ever reprinting of "Earth's Mausoleum," "Metamorphosis," and "Dark Eternity."

Three stories of soaring imagination, lost gems plucked from the pages of the pre-war issues of *Astounding Stories* during its "thought-variant" revitalization.

"Earth's Mausoleum" tells of interstellar visitors to Earth who seek to advance human civilization by conferring the benefits of their great science, but instead bring Earth to the brink of disaster.

"Metamorphosis" explores the terrifying aftermath of an ill-judged scientific experiment that destroys its creators and all life on Earth, and "Dark Eternity" is a fitting capstone to Fearn's "thought-variant" period, in which he destroys the entire universe!

THE GOLDEN AMAZON SAGA,
by John Russell Fearn

EARTH'SMAUSOLEUM

JOHN RUSSELL FEARN

Edited by Philip Harbottle

WILDSIDE PRESS

CONTENTS

INTRODUCTION

BY PHILIP HARBOTTLE

The revitalization of *Astounding Stories* brought about by new editor F. Orlin Tremaine in 1934 following his introduction of "thought-variant" stories, continued through 1935.

He was attracting all the best authors, including, inter alia, Stanley G. Weinbaum, John W. Campbell, Donald Wandrei, Murray Leinster. Eando Binder, Raymond Z. Gallun, C. L. Moore, Jack Williamson—and not least, John Russell Fearn.

Writing in an American fanzine in 1936, Fearn recalled:

> "1935 passed slowly in the early part then I got a bright idea about the moon and the rays of Tycho. The mystery of the moon's "bright streaks" has long fascinated me, so much so I wrote my own explanation of them and thus created "Earth's Mausoleum" published in the May 1935 *Astounding Stories*. Many readers said it was my best work, but I disagree with them."

This interesting story (Fearn's longest novelette to date) with its Howard Brown cover, and a double page splash interior illustration by Elliot Dold, has never been reprinted, a situation I am happy to redress. As Fearn indicated, it was very well received by readers, as typified by a letter from Ramon F. Alvarez Del-Rey ("Lester Del Rey"):

> "John Fearn did his best work for you in 'Earth's Mausoleum.' As usual, his science is not so hot, but that doesn't detract much from this story. I rate him a whole point higher after reading it."

Fearn's next five stories in *Astounding* have already been reprinted, or included in the body of later novels. "The Blue Infinity" (September 1935) was incorporated into a slightly expanded version as *The Renegade Star* (1952, and now scheduled as an E-book). The same scenario applies to "Mathematica" (February 1936) and "Mathematica Plus" (May 1936) which were included in an extended novel version as *To the Ultimate* (1952). The original versions of both stories are currently available in a Wildside collection *The Best of John Russell Fearn: Volume 1*, as is "Deserted Universe" (September 1936). "Dynasty of the Small" (November 1936) can be found in another Wildside collection, *Dynasty of the Small* (2012).

Our next uncollected story is "Metamorphosis" (January 1937). This dynamic novelette exemplifies Fearn's personal vision and conviction that the cinema was the ideal medium for science fiction.

Early in 1939, Fearn supplied two fascinating "about the author" essays to *Tales of Wonder* editor Walter Gillings, intended to accompany his reprinting of "The Man Who Stopped the Dust." Gillings then edited them into a very short (and rather bland) piece, unfortunately omitting some of Fearn's most interesting and revealing observations:

> "I am an undying believer in the power of the cinema to put science fiction over—but I certainly think we have been treated shabbily since *Things to Come*. Revival of horror films does not do a bit of good, and horror is a darn sight less probable than science. It is a source of unending mystery to me, and probably to a good few others, why producers should waste their time raking up bodies from the dead when there are thousands of first class stories in science just waiting for the cinema. The excuse that technical skill is lacking does not convince. It requires as much technique to put over horror as science—more, probably. Films are our best medium but when will producers see it?"

In "Metamorphosis" we find Fearn's cinematic imagination working at its best. Many of its scenes would later be closely copied for the cinema. Most striking of these were Fearn's "melting bodies" that were such a feature of *The Terminator* films, whilst his sentient rampaging electrical energies were later found in such films as Curt Siodmak's *Magnetic Monster* (1953) and Kurt Neuman's *Kronos* (1957).

Fearn's next stories in *Astounding* were "Worlds Within" (March, 1937), which can be found in Wildside's ebook collection, *The John Russell Fearn Science Fiction Megapack*, and "Penal World" (as Thornton Ayre, October, 1937) which can be found in Wildside's Fearn collection *World Without Chance* (2013).

Our final unreprinted Fearn story from *Astounding* is "Dark Eternity" (December, 1937), which was also Fearn's final thought-variant submission to Tremaine. But by the time it appeared, sporting a cover and interior illustrations by Hans Wesso, the magazine was being edited by John W. Campbell, who had taken over as editor in September 1937.

Fearn had continued to write for *Astounding* and Campbell, who bought another three stories in October—"Red Heritage," "The Mental Ultimate," "Whispering Satellite," and a fourth, "The Degenerates," in November.

The first three of these stories (as by Fearn, Polton Cross and Thornton Ayre) appeared in *Astounding*'s January 1938 issue, and "The Degenerates" (as Polton Cross) in February.

All four stories have been reprinted by Wildside. "Red Heritage" is available in Fearn's *SF Megapack*. "The Mental Ultimate" is included in *Rule of the Brains* (2012), and the remaining two can be found in *World Without Chance* (2013).

Following these acceptances Campbell had written to Fearn, who told Walter Gillings in a letter dated 9th January, 1938:

> "'Dark Eternity' marked the last thought-variant story I ever intend to write. Come to think of it, it was a fitting closing story to a long run of crazy scientific expositions. 'Red Heritage' marks the birth of the new Fearn, with a new style story,. Campbell has written me expressing his liking for this yarn and urges all future yarns be written in the same vein. Further (in confidence) he tells me that the

readers are swinging away from the heavy science thought-variant type of yarn to more interesting characters and lighter science. So I've changed my methods utterly. 'Red Heritage' was the start of the new method, and henceforth I shall change unrecognisably into the (in confidence) Polton Cross type of yarn…"

In point of fact, even if Campbell had not asked him to adopt a different style, it is difficult to see how Fearn could have come up with another thought-variant to follow "Dark Eternity." For in this story he *utterly destroys the entire universe and all creation!* How to follow that?

Although this present volume presents the first English language reprinting of "Dark Eternity," it is not widely known that the story had earlier been translated and published in a Japanese science fiction magazine in 1974. Nor that it had been chosen by SF historian and editor Mike Ashley to be included in his prestigious anthology *The Best of British SF: Volume 1 i*n 1977. However at the last moment (to Ashley's great annoyance) Futura's SF editor objected to the story and as Fearn's (and Ashley's) agent I was asked to find a replacement story. My replacement selection, which Futura found more acceptable, was "Alice, Where Art Thou?" (A story that can also to be found in Wildside's *The Best of John Russell Fearn: Volume 2*, 2002)

Ashley later went on the record: "…his (Fearn's) thought variants for *Astounding* all contained bold, original ideas." (*The Gernsback Years*, Wildside 2004).

In this he was echoing the earlier assessment made by the academic Frank Cioffi in his intriguing book *Formula Fiction? An Anatomy of American Science Ficrion 1930-194*0 (Greenwood, 1982):

> "Like other skilled authors working within the status quo format, Fearn pushes to extremes the extent to which reality is distorted and nearly destroyed; the extraordinarily inventive near-destruction his stories depict elevates them above the common run of routine, formula-based fiction.

"...the stories of Nat Schachner, Raymond Z, Gallun, John Russell Fearn, Stanton A. Coblentz, Donald Wandrei, and Leslie F. Stone are intelligent and entertaining, and deserve to be made accessible to today's vast SF audience."

Surely no fair-minded person reading this collection, and its predecessor volume *Before Earth Came*, would disagree!

EARTH'S MAUSOLEUM

I.

Norton Vane, assistant chief astronomer of the Vernwich Observatory of California, was singularly puzzled—indeed, more puzzled than he had ever been in his life before.

For quite twenty minutes he had been peering into the eyepiece of the new and stupendous lunar-refractor with which the observatory was equipped, and the longer he looked the more astonished he became. Then, presently, he disengaged his eye from the lens, blinked a trifle in the normal electric light, and resorted to considerable stroking of his chin.

"Astounding!" he commented at last, addressing the mute scientific instruments grouped about him. "The thing is unprecedented. I must find the doctor—"

With quick strides he left the immense observatory, passing through the connecting doorway into the research department. Here he found Dr. Hugo Konsicks, the presiding genius of the observatory, lately promoted to his high position by the American Institute of Science.

"Doctor! Doctor! The most amazing thing has happened!" Vane shouted. "You must come right away!

Konsicks looked up from the astronomical charts he was studying. His mild blue eyes, behind thick-lensed spectacles, surveyed the excited young astronomer with all the calm maturity of late middle age.

"What's the trouble, Norton?" he inquired, good-humoredly. "Has the Moon turned blue, or something? You seem pretty upset!"

"I am—and I have reason to be! The rays of Tycho, Copernicus, Kepler and Aristarchus have entirely disappeared! For the first time in the Moon's history!"

"What!" the doctor cried, leaping to his feet. "But—but that's impossible, boy! They're inseparable from the lunar surface—"

"No use in arguing, sir—they've gone," Vane returned tensely. "Even the smaller telescope we possess reveal that fact; with the giant telescope it's possible to see something peculiar existing in Tycho crater. A sort of chasm, Come and look."

"Assuredly I will! Most remarkable." The astronomer put his chart to one side and followed the younger man back to the lunar-refractor. Excitedly he took off his spectacles, then jammed his gaze to the eyepiece.

The view, to him, immediately became that of a portion of the Moon's brilliant surface, rendered viewable by semi-smoked glasses—the immense crater of Tycho filling all the view. Normally, it would have been a vision of blazing, reflected sunlight, with the strange phenomenon known as 'bright streaks and rays' fully in evidence. But tonight, for the first time in history, the rays were absent! Nor, as the refractor was moved to cover other portions of the Moon's surface, were there any streaks from the other salient 'radiation' points—Copernicus, Kepler and Aristarchus.

"You're right, Norton—the rays are missing!" Konsicks breathed. "And there is something else. Chasm of some sort— By Jove, yes—clean down the center of the crater floor!"

He withdrew his eyes and looked at Vane in dazed astonishment. In the same silence of profound puzzlement he replaced his spectacles, then, as though with a mute union of thought he and the young man moved to the balcony of the observatory into the open air, gazing with their unaided eyes at the full Moon, sailing high in the Californian night sky. Yet there was no apparent change. Truly the markings were more distinct owing to the removal of the bright streaks, but otherwise nothing was altered.

"What do you make of it, sir?" Vane asked at last, staring steadily upward.

"What am I to make of it?" Konsicks demanded almost impatiently. "You know as well as I do that those mysterious rays have been a feature of the Moon's face ever since man first looked at the heavens. Only at full Moon, as it is now, are these rays seen with any degree of clearness—one band extends, as you know, for seventeen hundred miles. Nothing has ever satisfactorily explained them—never explained how it is they pass through solid mountains; pass through everything and maintain a perfectly straight course. And cast no shadows!"

"Some experts say lava, doctor," the young man reminded him.

"Lava nothing!" The doctor's disgust was clearly manifest. "A stream of lava spreads out as it goes. It would form a lake on meeting a valley. These rays pass straight on over valley and hill alike, never once deflected. Nor can they be attributed to direct instead of oblique light, because at the edges of the Moon's apparent disk, on which the solar rays fall obliquely at full Moon, the brilliancy of the rays is the same." Konsicks paused and smiled faintly. "Funny to be reciting all this stuff, and now the rays have gone!" he muttered. "There's something unparalleled, something entirely strange and unsuspected, happening way up there, Norton. Come on—let's get back to the refractor."

The two returned to the observatory and the doctor resumed his observations of the satellite. Vane, chafing with impatience at being shut out, had to be content to listen to his superior's comments—breathless comments, stabbed out at intervals.

"Norton, there is something stirring in the depths of that chasm on Tycho's floor—I'm sure of it! In fact— Good heavens! Something is rising up resembling a submarine, as near as anything I can think of. Gleaming in the Sun—" Konsicks stopped and stared with all the intensity at his command, jealous of the faintest trace of mist on the lens, occasioned by his hard breathing.

The immense power of the instrument, the most powerful in the world, was capable of quite distinctly revealing any object above two feet in size on the lunar surface, so it was small wonder that Konsicks gazed dumbfounded at what he beheld. It went against all his scientific training and reasoning powers.

For a machine, of sorts, was indeed rising out of the chasm on the crater floor, until finally, after seeming to hover for a space, it came to rest on the floor itself. There was a long interval, and Konsicks waited patiently. Subconsciously he noticed that the rays of the Sun were now streaming down into the chasm itself; he decided it was curious he had not noticed it before. Had the Sun somehow brought this machine to life? Had the chasm been created on purpose? Certainly it had not existed hitherto.

"What's going on, sir?" It was Vane's voice, tense with excitement. "Tell me!"

A long pause followed, then Konsicks answered the question.

"My boy, either I am dreaming or going insane, but there are men—six of them—alighting from that machine! They seem to be—yes, they're wrapped up like divers; helmets and big boots and things. They seem to be pointing to something—maybe the Earth itself. Hello! They're going back inside the ship again now."

"Let me see—please!" Vane entreated.

"All right, but— No, wait a minute! The machine is moving off—going upward into space. Where the devil— Oh, yes, I see them again now, to the left. It's hard to follow them now. Damn! I've lost them! This instrument is too unwieldy to keep in line with them."

The astronomer withdrew his eye and looked at his assistant's eager face and bright eyes.

"A space ship, boy—from inside the Moon!" he exclaimed, his face amazed. "I always thought such things were too fantastic to be true. Yet here it is! On this memorable night of June 20, 1972. Perhaps—perhaps they are heading toward Earth. If so, at the rate they were traveling, they'll be here tomorrow night easily;"

"But where have they come from?" Vane demanded. "How in the name of wonder did they get inside the Moon? Do you think that perhaps they bored their way through from the other side—the side we never see?"

Konsicks shrugged. "How can I say? It's hardly likely. The Moon is a dead world all over so far as we know. Inside and out. Frankly, I don't know what to think! Other astronomers will surely have seen the lunar change—the breaking of the Tycho crater floor and the disappearance of the bright streaks. Just a moment; I'll ask Crespin at the New York Institute of Science. He'll be able to check up on us. I still think I must be suffering from delusions, or something."

He returned his glasses to his nose then crossed to the telephone. As was the custom in those advanced days, the connection was immediately made with the Institute. The voice of Reid Crespin, president of the Institute's astronomical section, came over the wire.

"You're not dreaming, doctor; it's an absolute fact! The Moon's face has changed for the first time in history. We saw the bright object leave its surface. Eh? Yes, it looked like a space ship, headed for Earth. Better inform the press."

"Do you think that's wise?" Konsicks asked quickly. "You know—ridicule, and so on. We'll never—"

"Don't worry!" Crespin replied firmly. "This has got to be believed. By tomorrow night, approximately, that ship will reach Earth, if it was headed here. I'll tell the press, People must be prepared for this."

"All right, if you think it's best," Konsicks returned. "Goodbye, Crespiti—and thanks."

Thoughtfully he hung up, and returned to Vane's side.

"Sir, suppose these people are visitors from space? Say—Lunarians?" the young man asked quickly. "Will the Earth be in danger?"

"They are not Lunarians or Selenites, whichever you call them. Those beings I saw were not at all adapted for life on the lunar globe. In appearance they were not unlike us—but considerably taller and broader. A Selenite would, according to all natural law, be somewhat insectile in appearance. Certainly not resembling us. No, Norton, I think those creatures really belong to a world not entirely dissimilar to ours, save that it is perhaps smaller, which would account for these creatures' greater size. But why do we worry? If they are coming, they will be here tomorrow, and they may have the most astounding tale in the universe to unfold. Something that will make us Earthlings realize our smallness. It will do good, too. If they are friendly, they can bestow innumerable benefits."

"If they are clever, they may be hostile," Vane muttered uncertainly.

"Why should they, my boy? That's rather a misguided conception. Cleverness, as a rule, begets friendliness—a desire and willingness to assist those of lesser intellect. Craving for power exists in those who think they are clever and really are not. But all this is needless conjecture. Tomorrow will show everything, if at all; I'm doing no more tonight; I'm too unbalanced. You can go home if you wish, Norton."

Vane accepted with alacrity. "Thanks, doc. I want to tell my wife all about this; she is interested in my work, you know. I shall live and wait for tomorrow. Good night, sir—I'll be here in the morning."

"Good night, Norton." The doctor smiled faintly at his enormous enthusiasm.

Vane went off with active strides, and as he made his way home, once he gained the level mountain road, his eyes were fixed on the Moon sailing serenely through the dark purple heavens. A Moon almost unchanged to the unaided eye, yet actually the strangest Moon that had ever looked down on Earth's busy, teeming surface.

Oddly enough, as he trudged onward—his bungalow was a mile and a half away—a lonely little place near the observatory—he began thinking of the numerous things blamed on the Moon. The tides, for one thing; spells of lunacy at full Moon for another, and above all the fantastic theories extended concerning the side never seen from Earth. As an astronomer he knew that the surface of the Moon never seen, if the whole was reckoned at 10,000 and the diurnal libration neglected, amounted to 4198. From that his thoughts traveled into the purely technical side of his profession, and he reached his home muttering remarks about the mean revolution of the nodes per annum and the mean advance of perigree— For twenty-seven years of age, Norton Vane was a brilliant young man, and a past master in mathematics.

He found his bungalow in darkness, as he had expected. After passing one more look at the satellite, then at the unending desert and remote mountain ranges that grouped about him in solemn majesty, he let himself in with his key and went silently into the bedroom.

With quiet insistence he shook his wife into wakefulness.

She sat up, blinking in the light of the bed lamp.

"Oh, it's you, Nort! For the moment you scared me—" She rubbed her eyes and peered at him under slumber-drugged lids. "What's the matter?" She yawned prodigiously. "Back early, aren't you?"

"Evelyn, the Moon has changed its face, lost its bright rays, and several men are coming from it to Earth. It happened tonight."

Evelyn, her soul, as ever, locked in her husband's work, became abruptly awake at that. With sudden energy she plied him with questions.

"It means something big, Eve," he concluded at last. "Earth is about to receive a visitation—and if there are any trips into space going free I'm in on one. I've always longed to see things above at really close quarters without the intervention of a lens."

"But what about me?" his wife pouted.

"You sweetheart? Well, what do you think? You'll come with me, of course if—"

"That would be wonderful," she admitted reflectively, then lay back and gazed through the window, the curtains being drawn to one side, toward the first hazy streaks of the newborn Californian day. Vane gripped her hand tightly for a moment, as though to emphasize the possibilities of the new day's arrival.

II.

During the night, authorized by Crespin of New York, the whole world's presses had been at work, and released upon a somnolent Earth the following morning the amazing news.

From New York to London, from London to Berlin, from Berlin via devious routes right across to the Antipodes to Sydney and Melbourne flashed the astounding message. The Moon had changed! Somewhere in the 240,000-mile gap between Earth and Moon was a space ship, bearing beings similar to Earthlings.

Those with astronomical tendencies held forth to their admiring families over the breakfast cups; those without such tendencies suddenly dug up information from all available sources, and textbooks on the Moon, formerly relegated to a back shelf in the public libraries of the world, suddenly became in insistent demand. In one instance, a Hollywood producer, the instant he heard the news, "killed" production on a revue epic and instead rushed through a scenario concerning, in prophecy, what might happen when the Selenites came. When informed the creatures were probably not Selenites at all, he merely became violent—

Strange indeed the way Earthlings took the news; how a flutter of excitement passed through every living soul on the planet. It changed thousands of people into confirmed scientists, and others into contemptuous scoffers. Dozens of weird contraptions sprang up overnight in various countries, principal among them being old-fashioned telescopes with which to view a quite invisible space ship, and so-called mathematicians who could tell exactly where the machine would land. A thousand and one weird professions sprang up to extract monetary gain from an egregious circumstance.

The general consensus of opinion was that the visitors would be dangerous, and would possess death rays, atom splitters, and deadly disease germs, which they would scatter indiscriminately over the Earth's surface. Speeches in this tempo, gleaned mainly from the stories in science-fiction magazines of that day, were made by soapbox orators, and succeeded in producing, before noon on that frenzied June 21, 1972, no fewer than twenty violent stampedes and riots in New York alone, and as many as forty-six in London. Life near these orators was at a premium. Had the orators in question possessed the slightest scientific knowledge things might have been less dangerous.

In the Vernwich Observatory, back in California, Dr. Konsicks and Vane spent an idle day. Their work was normally relegated to the night hours, but knowing what they did, they knew the night was liable, in this instance, to bring amazing happenings. The same tense anxiety existed at the New York Institute, and in the Greenwich Observatory in' London. All over the world every scientist and astronomer really worthy of his profession and calling was at his or her post, awaiting the moment when the visitors' space ship would be sighted.

Out at sea, under orders from the scientists, ships were specially searching, from their unimpeded viewpoint, the four corners of the heavens—but in the blaze of the summer day it was impossible to detect anything but the blue sky, of course. Even at night it would have been difficult enough, even with instruments, to detect that relative speck of microscopic dust in the firmament.

It was an amazing day in many ways—hot and thundery in those latitudes experiencing summer—cold and wet in others. Not in every place was the sky clear by evening time, and more than one amateur and professional astronomer gnashed his teeth in impotent fury at a cloudy sky.

It was almost dark when Vane left the observatory to snatch a brief supper at home and then return for the night. Here, in California, the evening was unimpaired. The clear and reliable climate showed promise of a perfect night. Vane felt curiously happy as he swung along; it always stimulated him to discover that something unusual was ahead of him. The prosaic and normal were anathema to him—hence his profession of astronomer which gave him the opportunity to explore the depths of space.

His wife had the supper ready when he entered, and she shot him a quick glance of expectation as, from long practice, he threw his hat upward to the peg on the door and watched it twirl round the hook into a resting position.

"Well, Nort, has anything happened?" She poured out his tea and handed it to him.

"Not yet. May happen any time, Eve; our calculations show that those visitors should have arrived some two hours ago. Evidently our figures were not entirely accurate."

She faced him across the table as he sat down.

"I've heard from the radio, Nort, that the most amazing things have been happening all over the world," she said slowly. "Just as though—as though everybody's going mad!" She laughed a trifle nervously. "There isn't anything to really be afraid of, is there?" she asked earnestly, her eyes full of wonder.

Vane set down his cup and smiled reassuringly. "My dear girl, do you think that all the scientists of Earth would be waiting so calmly to give our visitors a welcome if they were likely to prove dangerous? Of course not! You've been listening mainly to the reactions of an empty-headed world's population to a momentous occasion. That's all. Selenites, if such they are, don't come every day, sweetheart."

"Maybe that's just as well," Evelyn said reflectively; then brisking into action, "Here—take your choice! Cold meat, jelly, or trifle. You like trifle, Nort—"

She paused, forced into sudden silence, as her ear caught an alien sound. Vane heard it, too, at the same moment, and stopped stirring his tea to listen. It was a queer sound, somehow unexpectedly awesome in the warm silences of the desert that surrounded the astronomer's lonely abode.

It first obtruded into the ears as a thin whine, amazingly high up in the scale in pitch, but as the moments passed it crept slowly down until it became a decided humming—a humming that gained volume with the seconds.

"Quick!" Vane blurted out suddenly, dropping his spoon and hastily clutching his wife's arm. "It's the space ship—the Selenites! Come on—outside!" Without ceremony he hauled her, stumbling with the suddenness of it, to the doorway and outside. They both stood incontinently awe-struck at the sight that met their upward-turned gaze.

High in the almost dark sky, moving against the studded points of the stars with obvious tremendous velocity, was a brilliant gleaming mass. It was moving to neither right nor left, but directly forward, eating up distance and growing in dimensions with the moments. Over the desert hung that beating throb—the roar of tortured atmosphere.

"That's it—coming to Earth!" Vane gasped out, and his wife panted a quick exclamation.

Larger became the mass, and larger; louder grew the din, until it filled all space and every interspace. No engine whistle or volcanic steam could have made such an appalling din as the screech of the projectile machine through the air.

Then presently it came in a line with Earth's surface. It seemed to swing over suddenly to the left and came hurtling like a living mass of screaming flame toward the two in the doorway. Evelyn screamed in sudden fright, but Vane tightened his grip on her arm.

"Don't worry, Eve, it won't hit us. Watch! Good Lord, look!"

Straight over their heads, at an altitude of perhaps two thousand feet, shot the mammoth machine, every inch of three hundred feet in length, and tapering to both ends. It seemed to be surrounded by a mass of radiating rays and streaks, and as it passed directly above, those same rays beat down for a trice within a yard or two of the astronomer and his wife. Instantly they were flung off their feet and hurled on their faces into the sand of their small garden. Grains shot through the air; the tumult of a hot and blistering wind enveloped them and pressed them flat. Grilling heat hemmed them in.

Out of the corner of his eye, as he struggled to rise, Vane noticed that everywhere those radiating rays were touching, sand and shrubs were flying into dust and nothingness. Even where the solid mass of the mountain ranges were flicked, the rocks blew into a thousand fragments as though dynamited with super-explosive. Then, with a roar, the monster shot to Earth beyond the nearby range, but a radiating mass of snow-white rays pouring into the darkness of the sky revealed where it had fallen.

Dazed and bewildered, Vane struggled to his feet, dragging his startled wife up beside him. Together they looked away to the left where lay the white radiance of rays, the mountain range silhouetted in front of them.

"Well, Evelyn, the visitors are here," he said, his voice grim. "I don't know whether they're hostile or not, but beyond doubt they're radiating something from that ship of theirs that blows ordinary rocks into fine ash. I guess if those rays had fallen directly on us, instead of a few yards away, we wouldn't be talking now."

"They're hostile, Nort," Evelyn said, her brow wrinkled. "They've got dangerous weapons aboard."

"It depends," Vane replied reflectively. "They might have been repulsive radiations to ward off brickbats and things in outer space. Until we've personally seen the invaders we can't tell. The thing to do is to follow them up. Looks as though they have landed about thirty miles away. Come on—I must tell the doctor right away, if he doesn't already know."

"Nort! Let me come with you—please!"

"Eh?" He considered briefly, then nodded. "All right, come on. It's unethical—but then this is an unethical occasion. I'll get the car out while yoij slip some things on. Bring my hat with you."

The girl went into the bungalow and Vane went round to the small garage adjoining it. Fifteen minutes later he and Evelyn were bumping along the uneven mountain road toward the observatory, their eyes flashing ever and again to that criss-crossing mass of rays and beams beyond the mountains, far more powerful than any known Earthly searchlight. For some odd reason the memory of the rays of Tycho kept returning to Vane's subconscious mind.

Dr. Konsicks had not only seen the space ship's arrival, but was preparing to depart on foot when Vane arrived. He accepted the invitation to go by car with alacrity and seated himself in the rumble-seat, passing comments, during the bumpy journey, upon the possibilities ahead.

Once the desert road was gained, the going was harder still, but knowing the district so well, Vane was able to take the nearest cuts across the hard, sun-blistered sand roads, until he struck the roadway of the second mountain range, some forty-five minutes later. Fifteen minutes more would bring them to the crest of the road where they would be able to see the visitors. The pulses on three people beat faster than normal as a result of this speculation.

Then, as they were nearing the summit of the road, the rays, which had been blazing over the mountain range far above them, suddenly flickered fitfully and went out. Darkness descended save for the light of the rising Moon, just past her fullest phase.

"Just what would happen!" Vane grunted, driving on steadily by the light of the headlights. "Wonder why they've done that?"

The doctor passed no comment; he seemed to be thinking—but he strained forward eagerly over Evelyn's shoulder as the top of the road was gained. In the valley below lay one of the westernmost points of the Yuma Desert, still and silent in the gathering Moonlight. Or so it appeared at first—then, as another bend was rounded, there became visible a faintly glittering monstrosity lying still and dark in the sand, for all the world like a land submarine, if there were such a thing.

"That's it!" Vane shouted excitedly, shutting off the engine and bringing the car to a standstill. "What do we do, doc? Go and look it over?"

"Let's!" Evelyn implored eagerly. "Why not?"

Konsicks shrugged; his eyes seemed a trifle dubious behind their thick lenses.

"Well, since we've come so far, there's no reason why we shouldn't at least—eh—look it over," he answered. "But keep your distance; we don't know what we may encounter."

As excitedly as children on a picnic, Vane and his wife clambered out, assisting the more staid and mature doctor after them. Then, with cautious steps they made their way through the loose sand toward the apparently lifeless monster. They wished they could detect some sign of life—a light, or something. The sudden cessation of the rays and the silence was somewhat disconcerting when so much had been expected.

"Guess it looks like a fizzle," Vane grunted, when they had approached to within a hundred feet of the vessel. "Nothing doing! It isn't hot through passage through the atmosphere, which in itself is a mystery. We'd better wait till daylight, doc."

"Perhaps you're right," Konsicks agreed. "Certainly we—"

He broke off in mid-sentence and stood transfixed as, with a suddenness that left no chance of escape, there blazed from the silent ship a brilliant white beam. In an instant it had enveloped the three adventurers in its blinding light.

They staggered back, arms raised to their faces.

"Run for it!" Vane gasped out suddenly. "We're spotted! We're—" He broke off, blinking in the intolerable glare, as he abruptly found himself facing an individual who had appeared with utter silence from the darkness beyond the searchlight's radius.

"Oh!" gasped Evelyn in alarm, catching sight of him at the same moment.

Dr. Konsicks said nothing; his mild blue eyes were filled with plain surprise.

The man, for such he appeared to be, was perhaps seven feet six or eight inches in height and of proportionate width. His attire seemed to consist of tight-fitting leg coverings and a loose, much-embroidered smock. Head covering he had none. Fortunately, the face was not of a ruthless or cruel type, but rather one of good-humored tolerance and understanding, yet withal powerful and firm. Altogether a fine-looking creature, with his extremely hooked nose, high cheek bones, and, surprisingly enough, red eyes and snow-white hair, akin to an Albino. Certainly his white hair was not occasioned by considerable age, for he appeared young.

For a long time this remarkable person looked at the three in complete silence, then he raised his arm and pointed, presumably in the direction of the space ship.

"Go on," muttered Konsicks. "I think we can trust him." Cautiously, as though expecting something startling to happen any moment, Vane led the way, Evelyn clinging to his arm. The doctor came up in the rear, followed by the giant with the red eyes. As the party moved, the searchlight followed them, until Vane found himself walking into an area where the light was more tolerable. He moved slowly now, amazed at what he beheld, turning to read the same expressions of wonderment on the faces of his wife and Konsicks. The astronomer himself was peering through his glasses with the earnestness of a bird on a wet garden lawn.

Came a clicking sound; the door had shut. The three looked about them at the well-lighted apartment of metal in which they found themselves—an apartment stacked with mainly incomprehensible machines and devices from end to end, besides which the control room of a submarine would have seemed the veriest child's nursery.

The giant with the red eyes motioned to an affair resembling a ship's bunk, and in response the three Earthlings sat down. The visitor vanished into an adjoining apartment, to return shortly with five companions, all remarkably similar to himself in appearance; but from his manner he was clearly the leader. Then, at last, he spoke, in a deeply melodious bass voice, raising his arm at the same time in the manner of a salute.

"Mori hanji voonar!" said his profound voice.

"That's Greek to us," Vane responded. "We don't understand your language, chief, nor you ours, I suppose. What are we going to do about it?"

The man's bright-red eyes became thoughtful, then he tapped his mighty chest, afterwards pointing to Vane. Several times he repeated the action before it dawned on the young astronomer what was implied.

"He means will I teach him the language!" he exclaimed, turning to the others. "How about it, doc? Shall we try?"

"Surely," Konsicks assented. "Your wife and I will assist. The sooner we get the language difficulty over, the sooner we'll know something about all this."

So began the first bridging between two worlds. By pointing to various objects and supplying the Earthly word for them, the three managed, little by little, to impart their language to the huge visitors. They proved to be amazingly quick to grasp every detail, and once they heard a word they never forgot it. In all, it was a task that took only seven Earthly hours—until the summer dawn, in fact. In that time all six men knew enough to talk with perfect fluency, whereas the Earthlings had barely gained the rudiments of the visitors' language. Obviously, the mental powers of the giants were some three times greater than an average clever Earthling.

Weary but successful, the three were able to relax at last, and with that the leader motioned his comrades from the apartment into an adjoining one.

"First, my friends, let me extend to you our friendship," he said quietly. "My name is Mayro. We do not come as enemies, intent on ruining, conquering or stealing your planet; rather we would like to bestow our knowledge upon you. For a space of roughly ten ages we have been asleep, in a state of suspended animation, in that mighty mausoleum known as your Moon. So be it, then. We ourselves, inside this space ship, have slept within your Moon ever since your Earth was just beginning to cool."

"What's that?" demanded Konsicks, rising up as the import of the visitor's words penetrated his brain. "What did you say?"

Mayro smiled and repeated his statement. Vane and Evelyn listened in silent but deeply interested curiosity. "It is a strange story—perhaps the strangest ever told," Mayro went on pensively. "I will tell it to you.

"Countless ages ago—the exact time I cannot remember—I set out from my native planet with my companions—my planet being situated in a galaxy some forty thousand light years beyond your nearest star—on a tour of space exploration. We had been masters of space travel for many ages, so it was nothing new to us—but we were always trying to explore farther and learn more. On this occasion, due to a defect in one of our guiding compasses, we lost our way in space. We wandered about the cosmos, completely lost, and wondering if perhaps death would not be the best way out. Then it chanced that our wanderings brought us to a cosmic birth; we saw the birth of your solar system and its nine planets, and our course brought us, when Earth had cooled down into a semisolid state, to your planet.

"My comrade, Zanos, suggested that instead of death, it might be more interesting for us if we waited until the world of Earth bore men upon its surface. We could drive our space machine deep down into the depths of the Earth and use the repulsive forces of our ship's metal to keep away the pressure of hardening soil and rock. You see, the metal of which this ship is composed normally emits perpetual energy, in the form of brilliant rays, which are actually force—something akin to your radium. When these rays are in action the metal becomes transparent, but the application of a current, which is on now, stops both the rays and the transparency, turning the metal into an inert opacity. You understand?"

"Yes, yes," Konsicks nodded eagerly. "Go on! Did you bury yourselves?"

"Assuredly we did. We drove our ship deliberately into the depths of the soft, moist world, and then switched off our metal current. That meant our metal became immediately repulsive and surrounded us with an area of unbreakable force, so we could never be crushed by surrounding forces. Ultimately, we realized, the surface above us would spilt in two under the enormous strain from below, but not before millions of years had passed. We knew this would occur—figures proved it—and we knew also that our metal had a life of some twenty million of your years before it lost its powers, so we decided, until that time should come, we would place ourselves in a state of suspended animation. But, once the ground above us cracked, allowing the Sunshine to reach us through the transparent walls of our ship, an automatic instrument would react at the Sunlight and actuate a spring, setting forth a compressed air cylinder, preserved through unguessable centuries by the ultimate of cold, within a vacuum. So, slowly the temperature would rise by the Sunlight and the air would come as well. We would awake—we *did* awake.

"We arose from our condition—a condition that was death, yet life. Before we had succumbed, the air had been entirely pumped out of our chamber, our ship, and machines had reduced our mental and physical vibrations to almost zero. After we had relapsed into that long sleep, automatic machines had reduced the temperature of the ship to 273.1 degrees on our Centigrade thermometer—the cold of space itself. Then, as I have said, we awoke again, but our tests revealed there was no air outside our ship, and that the temperature was that of 98 marones, or five hundred of your Farenheit degrees! What in the cosmos had happened? This was anything but what we had calculated.

"Deeply puzzled, we donned space suits, capable of standing extremes of heat and cold and airlessness, and raised our machine through the chasm our repulsions had made, to find ourselves in an immense crater. We found a light gravitation, a dead world, a sun from which the prominences streamed and round which hung the halo of the pearly corona—and above all a gigantic world, not very far across the void, obviously alive and possessing clouds and atmosphere. For a time the mystery baffled us, then we began to understand. By some amazing mischance, which we had never reckoned with, we had imbedded ourselves in the portion of the still hardly cooled Earth which ultimately must have broken off and become the Moon. We felt nothing during that wild transit across space; our radiations protected us, and our ship was likewise impervious to heat or cold. All the violent convulsions the Moon had gone through during her cooling period also had left us untouched for the same reason. So you may imagine our dismay at finding ourselves on a dead world—Earth's mausoleum, indeed. You never guessed six men from the cosmos lay within the moon, did you?" Mayro's face creased in a broad smile.

"Never," Konsicks returned with conviction. "I begin to understand at last. The bright rays and streaks from Tycho and other points, Vane, were obviously caused by the radiations of the buried space ship. That is why they were not blocked by anything solid—I presume they're not?" he asked, looking up.

"Correct," Mayro assented. "Although they repulse, they pass through all solids—or at least the light part of the emanations do. The actual emanations themselves block a solid, of course. Resist it, so to speak."

"Which explains why the radiations vanished when you awoke," Konsicks went on thoughtfully. "The radiations must have got through the weakest parts of the Moon's surface—Tycho and so forth, and ultimately broke the floor of Tycho crater in two. That permitted Sunlight to stream down, pass through the transparent walls of the ship and wake you. Then you switched on the electric current which caused the rays to vanish and your ship to become opaque. Then you came to Earth, rays in full blast—"

"Certainly our radiations were in action," Mayro assented. "We use them for the dual purpose of propulsion and repulsion of unwanted bodies. These same radiations also prevent friction from atmosphere and keep our ship cool. Perhaps we caused a little damage when we were landing, but that was unavoidable. We chose this desert as it seemed the quietest spot. Our last wish is to injury anybody. All we desire is to see what sort of a world evolved out of the solar gas we once saw. Manifestly it has bred intelligent creatures, though it must be admitted you are not so high in intellect as we are. Perhaps we can help you? We came with that object in view."

Konsicks considered, then glanced at Vane and Evelyn.

"That's kind of you, Mayro, but— Well, you see, we Earthlings are a conservative sort of race. We resent interference, or being taught anything. I do not mean that we three personally are that way—rather the contrary—but I speak of those who are not scientific, of the great masses, which unfortunately comprise the vast majority of our Earthly population."

The giant nodded slowly, that faint smile once more appearing on his powerful face.

"I think I understand, friend Konsicks. Still, your races would surely be interested in the colonization of the Moon?"

"Colonization?" Vane repeated in amazement. "You talk of colonizing a dead world?"

Mayro shrugged. "It is dead by natural standards, I agree, but science can very soon revive it and transform it into quite a useful annex to the Earth. I have to admit my surprise that it has not been already done, but obviously, since you know no way to cross space, you have literally arrived at a dead end. We can colonize the Moon for you—nor is that all we can do. We can bestow upon you many useful gifts from our own scientific knowledge."

"Such as?" inquired Konsicks curiously. "We have radio, you know. And television."

"Useful, but commonplace," returned Mayro calmly. "Such things as cold light, the transference of matter, the transmutation of elements, the harnessing of the tides and the control of the weather may also interest you. You can have all those gifts if you desire them."

Konsicks got slowly to his feet; he surveyed Mayro steadily.

"Mayro, I am an Earthling," he said quietly. "Inborn in me are the traditions and instincts of my race. One of the unwanted traits in an Earthling's make-up is to be suspicious. That is just what I am now. You offer all these scientific marvels to us, but it is only natural that you demand a price in return."

The visitor shook his huge head. "For a man of science, friend Konsicks, you reveal a surprising limitation of knowledge. We ask no price! We are wanderers from space—lost, our world by this time dead and airless. In return for only the safety of your planet; in return for the leisurely study of Earthlings without in any way interfering with them, we offer you our knowledge. Nothing more—nothing less. I have five companions, as you are aware, and all have no intention of hostility. We can, of course, defend ourselves when attacked, and tolerate no injustices or wrongdoing, but of ourselves we are never the aggressors. We come—as friends!"

Konsicks hesitated at that and glanced at the intent Vane and Evelyn. Vane nodded earnestly to signify his approval of the visitor's offer.

"Well—er—I am in rather an awkward position," the doctor said. "Really, you are placing me in the light of Earth's ambassador, which is too mighty a responsibility to rest entirely on my shoulders. My suggestion is that all six of you accompany us to the New York Institute of Science. It is the greatest institution of its kind on our planet, and deals with all branches of science. The head of the astronomical section, Reid Crespin, is a personal friend of mine—a man of broad views, penetrating brains, and absolute fearlessness. If anybody can make the world believe in you, he can! He knew of your coming, just as we did. We happened to be nearest; that's why we came first."

"I understand," the giant nodded. "Our detectors showed us somebody was near our vessel; that was why we switched on the searchlights. It was the first time we had ever seen Earthlings. Strange you should resemble us, though on a smaller scale. In all, we have visited some five hundred and eighty planets in our travels, and not a single one has held life resembling our own. It is fortunate that in face and body formation, at least, we are similar. But I digress, my friends. We will visit this Crespin right away."

"I would suggest a little later, when the day has fully come," Konsicks said. "My companions and I are tired; teaching you the language was a strain on us. Besides, we sleep at night."

Mayro shrugged, then crossed to one of the six windows in the wall and snapped back a metal shutter. The vision was one of steadily approaching day across the emptiness of the desert.

"It is nearing day," he commented. "Still, we will go when you desire it. Return to your abodes and come back when you are refreshed. We have no wish to overstrain you."

Konsicks stifled a yawn. "We'll do that, then. We'll be back by mid-afternoon when we have eaten and slept a little. In the meantime, guard yourselves against sight-seers. Plenty will be along, I expect."

The giant nodded as he opened the door of the vessel. "Have no fear, Konsicks. We know how to protect ourselves. We shall eagerly await your return."

III.

It was toward three in the afternoon before the three returned to the visitor's space ship, refreshed with brief sleep and a meal—and, as they had anticipated, a fair-sized crowd of people was gathered round the monster, talking and pointing excitedly.

"Just what I expected!" Vane grunted. "Why the devil can't people keep their noses out?"

"A space ship doesn't fall every day Norton," Dr. Konsicks answered. "Come—we will have to force our way through."

This proved to be a task more difficult in practice than speech. The sightseers certainly did not believe that the three newcomers were acquainted with the unknown and as yet unseen creatures inside the ship; they merely suspected, humanlike, that they desired a closer view, and as a consequence the three unwittingly let themselves in for a good deal of rough handling. The crowd was mostly composed of a hooligan element—unimaginative young men and women who had been willing to brave the rocky roads of hill and dale for the sake of stimulating their curiosity.

As yet, no experts had arrived on this out-of-the-way spot. Probably because the ship's location had not been fully determined. It was as they neared the space ship that Evelyn was suddenly knocked to the ground by an aggressive brute of a fellow, head and shoulders above the small knot of 'toughs' who were obviously his companions, upon whose foot she happened to tread. Vane wheeled round, eyes glittering, and retracted his arm for a blow—but before he could land it another rough behind him sent him spinning. Dr. Konsicks stooped down to help the fallen and frightened girl, but he, too, was legged down.

"Say, grandpa, what's the big idea?" the massive hooligan demanded. "Thought you'd get a good look, huh?"

"You infernal blackguard!" Konsicks shouted furiously. "How dare you—"

"Aw, shut up! Any more from you and we'll—"

"You will what?" inquired a deep bass voice from behind the hooligan's ear—and he spun round, fists clenched, to do battle with the new aggressor. It came as a violent shock to him, however, to find the creature was nearly twice as broad and head and shoulders taller. Eyes of bright red, filled with a light of intense fury, were glowing strangely.

With one surging movement the crowd fell back, chattering nervously. How the giant had arrived nobody could quite make out; he had just—come.

"Mayro!" Vane gasped thankfully "Thank goodness you've come along." He helped his fallen wife up and dusted the sand from her clothes. "This damned hooligan here—"

"I saw everything," returned Mayro's calm voice. "We are a peaceful people, Earthling"—this to the dazed hooligan—"but when you interfere with our friends it is then that you anger a race who could, if necessary, exterminate you into fine powder at a second's notice! That is not my way; you are the first offender, therefore I shall at least spare your life. You did, however, cause this Earthly lady and her husband quite unnecessary pain; therefore, I shall repay you in your own coin. It will perhaps teach you a lesson."

"Look here—" the man began savagely.

"Like this!" Mayro added calmly, and with a suddenness that was devastating he flung out his right fist with the speed of a lightning bolt. The result was truly astounding. The blow struck the scowling hooligan under the jaw, and such was the terrific force of the giant's biceps that it lifted him, powerful man though he was, clean off his feet. He turned a complete drunken somersault through the air and crashed down with his face in the sand, utterly winded, and no doubt suffering from a broken jaw.

"Excellent," Mayro said in satisfaction. "Now, my friends, come inside." He escorted the three into the ship and securely locked the door behind them.

"Mayro, you shouldn't have done that—decent though it was of you," Vane exclaimed. "Hooligans like that are the last type to inflame to violence. If that fellow has a strong following, and he seems to have plenty of colleagues, he might do some damage."

The giant laughed softly. "You need have no fear, my friends. There is nothing on this planet that can interfere with us. I trust our aggressive enemy has suffered for his behavior."

"How in the world did you know all about it?—arrive so quietly?" Konsicks asked curiously.

"Merely the transference of matter, which I mentioned last night. In the first place, I saw your treatment via our periscopic devices, and also heard the altercation through our sound-wave apparatus. That being so, I did the same as last night—I projected myself by an automatic machine, requiring no operator, into the crowd. It is quite a simple process—to us. A body is rotated into hyperspace, moved for any given distance through all solids, and then made to materialize again at the desired point.

"Everything is determined beforehand—the distance and so forth—and the setting of the machine at the commencement saves any operator having to bother it while the transmission is made.

"Anybody can go anywhere by that process. I often use it; saves a lot of time, particularly in difficult situations."

Mayro paused and looked about him, nodded toward his five white-haired companions who had just entered the control room. "We are ready for the departure to friend Crespin," he remarked.

"Right," said Konsicks. "I told Crespin you'd be coming—be there about nightfall, I said—depending on your vessel's speed. I said you'd go in the ship; is that all right?"

"Perfectly—granting there is somewhere we can land."

"Crespin is having the Institute grounds cleared for you. There'll be ample room."

"Excellent! We will start at once."

Mayro turned to his colleagues and gave brief orders. In response they turned to the complicated control panels and busied themselves with numberless switches and levers, their red eyes glued to the strange meters on a level with their great height.

"What about the people below?" asked Vane suddenly, in alarm. "If you're using your radiations, you'll kill them and—"

"Have no fear, friend Vane. For normal flight through the air we do not use our radiations. Purely a system by which we adhere immovably to the electric waves that are eternally passing through every atmosphere, which have seeped down from the electro-magnetic ether beyond. That makes a fall impossible, and also provides enormous momentum. Our only need is a recoiling power which is generated from a copper bar at either end of the ship, depending on the direction of travel. I believe you use the antiquated system of a propeller— Ah! We are on our way. Come to the window; you must guide our route."

From the main observation window the three Earthlings looked down on the milling crowd below, the majority pointing skyward. Some had fallen over with the terrific back draft; still others were shaking their fists at the fast receding ship. Vane and Konsicks—and Evelyn, too, in a lesser degree—had an uneasy feeling that a very inimical start had been made with Earth's only too-temperamental people.

"How far is this New York?" asked Mayro presently.

"Some three thousand miles," Konsicks answered. "How long will it take you?"

"Oh, roughly thirty of your minutes," came the astonishing answer. "I must apologize for the slowness. Were we in space, unimpeded, we could be there almost instantaneously. Even here we could be in New York instantaneously by the transference of matter, but I think it better that Earthlings see our ship as well as us."

"Thirty minutes!" Vane expostulated. "Why—that's six thousand miles an hour!"

"Exactly so. Trifling indeed compared to the speeds at which we can cross space. We took a very leisurely journey from Moon to Earth. When speed is really necessary, we can easily reach the speed of light, and once we attained a velocity of nearly 744,000 miles a second, which is four times light's velocity."

A silence fell at that. The matter-of-fact way in which Mayro remarked upon incomprehensible speeds was a little too much for the Earthlings to grasp. They allowed the matter to drop and contented themselves in marveling at the smoothness with which the ship hurtled onward through the air, already well over the arid regions of New Mexico.

So onward with undiminished speed across Kansas and Missouri—until at last Indiana, Ohio and Pennsylvania had passed beneath. At times there were glimpses of people staring upward from the streets, though it was probable that everybody knew what it was all about—and in New York itself it was obvious that all people were aware of the coming of the visitors.

Surrounding the immense grounds of the Institute of Science, west of the metropolis, was a mass of people as far as the eyes could reach, held back by lofty iron railings and an army of mounted and foot police. From end to end of the great city the news had spread, thanks to Konsicks' message to Crespin, of the coming of the creatures from the cosmos, who so long had been buried in the mausoleum of the Earth, as Mayro insisted on poetically terming ft.

The space ship alighted softly on the grounds and came to a standstill. When the door was opened the roaring of the people smote like something solid from the boundaries. Mayro stood looking about him for a moment, then his eyes lighted on a small deputation approaching steadily.

"It's Crespin himself," Konsicks remarked, moving forward. "He's got radio and television transmitters with him, too. See those men bringing them up in the rear? You're going to be shown to the world already, Mayro."

"Why not?" asked the giant quietly. "The sooner the better, I imagine."

Presently Crespin came up, flanked on either side by the television experts, the newsreel and newspaper men, and several governmental officials and scientific representatives.

"You are Mayro?" Crespin asked, his lean face full of affability.

"That is so," conceded the visitor calmly, then motioned to his racial companions. "These are my comrades— Zanos, Liret, Venor, Balo and Kisnad, Behind them are my Earthly friends."

"Quite so," Crespin nodded, and subdued a smile as he beheld the reporters' shorthand struggles with the unusual names. "In the name of the United States, and in the name of the planet Earth, Mayro, we welcome you to our planet and city. We have learned the,basis of your plans from Dr. Konsicks of California, and now await your own personal verification. Will you give a televised and radio address to the people of the world tonight, from the Institute of Science?"

"Willingly," Mayro nodded. "While I am on this world, it is my desire—and that of my comrades—to conform to your standards of living. We will make the Institute our headquarters for the time being."

"You will be treated as honored guests," Crespin replied. "Will you accompany us to the Institute, where a banquet has been prepared?"

"Does a banquet include Earthly foods?" Mayro asked doubtfully, and on being told it did he shook his head slowly. "I am sorry, but we must withdraw from that. We only use specially prepared substances, by injection. We will come—but not to eat."

Crespin shrugged. "Entirely as you wish. Come along, gentlemen—all of you; and to you, Dr. Konsicks, belongs the honor of being the first to discover the change on the moon."

"No—to Norton Vane here," Konsicks quickly corrected, and at that Vane smiled somewhat shyly for the battery of cameras and patted his wife's clinging arm reassuringly.

Then, the entire party, visitors and visited, moved slowly and sedately toward the mighty square bulk of the Institute of Science.

At nine o'clock, the banquet over, Mayro turned his attention to the broadcasting room with which the Institute was equipped, and, under Crespin's directions, took his stand before the television transmitter and microphone.

For nearly three quarters of an hour he dealt solely with his experiences prior to the awakening of himself and his comrades within the Moon—then passed on to his offer of scientific knowledge in return for the safety of the Earth. "...under our directions, if you are willing to follow them out, we can colonize the Moon, control Earth's weather, harness the tides, and accomplish countless new improvements. The benefits would be incalculable."

"Of what exact use would it be to colonize the Moon, Mayro?" Crespin asked.

"An extra planet if rendered habitable, is surely useful?" Mayro asked in polite surprise. "Think of the extra room there will be on Earth. This world is much overcrowded. Your unemployment problem, too, is considerable. Annexing the Moon would reduce that unemployment, and further ideas we have in mind would indeed render unemployment a thing of the past."

"Well, it is entirely up to the world's peoples to decide the issue," said Crespin. "For myself, I give my unhesitating assent, but you men and women watching and listening now"—he turned to the transmitters—"are the grand-jury in this matter. All I can say is, show yourselves to be generous to our visitors, and in return we will reap a rich harvest. Don't be afraid to admit that there are people cleverer than yourselves; that the knowledge that has come out of cosmos is far and away greater than anything we have ever attained yet—"

So, practically on that note, ended the broadcast, and half an hour later the visitors returned to their space ship, closed the impregnable doors, and vanished for the night from the eyes of the surging populace around the grounds of the edifice, struggling and fighting desperately to gain a glimpse of the men who were going to change the earth.

* * * *

For a week after the tele-broadcast, Earthlings squabbled and bickered among themselves, like children over a ball, concerning the visitors' offer. Opinions were conflicting in every direction, but curiously enough it was the gigantic problem of the world-unemployment, still rife even in those advanced days of 1972, that decided the issue.

To accept Mayro's proposal would mean employment for tens of thousands of men and women, skilled and unskilled—so, with due formality, there ultimately came from every country's presiding government or dictator an official sanction, plastered with seals, for the visitors to proceed with their plans. Followed much signing upon strips of tough parchment, and the appending of monstrous masses of sealing wax to silk ribbons, all of which Mayro and his comrades viewed with faintly amused interest.

They failed utterly to comprehend such legal procedure, but were too polite to pass comment.

The day the acceptance of the visitors became world-wide, Vane, Evelyn and Konsicks joined Crespin and the visitors in the main laboratory of the Institute. A few outsiders were present, mainly government representatives who would take the first orders from Mayro.

"Firstly, we will harness the sea and do away with your foolish power houses," Mayro said complacently.

"That has already been done," Crespin answered promptly. "In some parts, tide mills are used to create power where tidal action is considerable. A basin is flooded twice a day and drives a mill wheel with a small head. The only drawback is that the power is intermittent, of course, and comes at different times of the day."

"Quite! An elementary version of the real thing, friend Crespin. On our world we used to harness the sea perpetually. We had approximately seven thousand rotating spindles, not unlike gigantic screws in shape, all along the shores of our principal oceans. These screw bars revolved perpetually with the waves and went out far enough to reach low tide—so at high and low water the waves were perpetually giving a driving power since they always moved the same way. Farther back from the shore reposed a power house, and the combined energy of the seven thousand rotating screws was synchronized by various machines, and then passed into the power transformers. Thence by wires to the various centers requiring power. That is what we will do along Earthly coasts, my friends. Power for nothing! You have very little conception what enormous resources and facilities lie in a world's own natural properties."

"True," Crespin nodded thoughtfully; then looking up, "You said something, too, about weather control."

"Similarly simple. Weather conditions are produced by constantly changing pressures and electric charges in the atmosphere. The correct electric radiations, released from immense power houses—driven by the tides themselves—will keep the pressures in the atmosphere on a level keel, and can be altered at will to produce either rain or sun as desired. The transference of matter I have already explained to you. The colonization of the Moon is the biggest project. It will be necessary for an expedition to visit the Moon in space ships, which will be built on similar lines to ours, only much larger. We will take with us all the material necessary. To decide on those materials will of necessity take some little time, and in any case I do not plan to undertake the colonization for a year. It will take me that long to make the necessary terrestrial improvements."

Crespin nodded. "Very well, Mayro. You are, as you know, virtually in control of the Earth and its peoples. Everything is in your hands, in the matter of future progress, anyhow. If you can model a useful world out of the formless clay you have to go on, all power to you! Eh, Vane?" The young astronomer nodded emphatically.

"You will, I suppose, select certain people to aid you?" Dr. Konsicks asked.

"Of course. You, doctor, shall be my closest adviser on Earthly matters, of which, as yet, I am mainly ignorant. You, Vane—and your wife—will be extremely useful in positions of authority. You can do much with the men; your wife with the women. And to you, Crespin, will also be extended a similar authority. Indeed, when the departure is made for the Moon you will be the one I shall hope to leave in my place, in charge of Earth's peoples."

"Suits me," Crespin answered with a faint smile. "And now let's get to business. The world is waiting to see something."

"The world *will* see something," Mayro returned with conviction. "Have no fear of that, friend Crespin!"

IV.

So, onward from that memorable day, began the vast improvement in the constructional scheme of the world. The visitors, headed by Mayro, went about their plans with ordered and patient infallibility, never once causing the slightest friction, always willing to listen to suggestions for alteration—but crushing needless slackness and bad workmanship with a relentless hand.

The outcome of it all was a changed and unrecognizable world twelve months later.

The One-Year Plan was perfected to the day—on August 10, 1973—and, had a visitor been in space for that year, he would certainly have thought he had landed on a different planet to the one which he left, so changed was the new Earth from the old.

Disintegrators and assemblers had done away with all the old cities. London, New York, Paris—every principal city—had been moved with speed and efficiency, literally rayed out of existence. In their places reposed cities in the sky, built upon colossal platforms, rearing some five hundred feet from the ground. The vast pillars of incorrodible steel supporting the cities were sunken into revolving turntables far beneath the Earth, balanced to perfection, and able to turn when necessary by electricity—in order to have constant sunlight—which electricity was generated from the stupendous power houses that utilized the natural energy of the nearest ocean!

Connecting these sky cities were suspension bridges, able to fold or extend at will. Thus had mankind suddenly taken to the freedom and dustlessness of the sky, leaving below perfectly free ground space, which was utilized for high-speed vehicular traffic, able now to take the shortest routes being unimpeded by buildings. In every quarter, too, particularly in business, the hyperspace matter transferor was in great demand, mainly for the time it saved.

In the earlier days of storms and uncertain weather the sky cities would have been destroyed within a few months, but now, thanks to the faultless weather-controlling machines installed the world over, the weather always maintained a perfect calmness—giving way to soft rain or sharp frosts at the desired times. Gales and thunderstorms were forgotten nightmares that once terrorized the seaman and ruined the farmer.

Beneath the Earth had been tunneled an enormous underground railway, just under the Earth's crust, through which hurtled streamlined trains at a speed of nearly three hundred miles an hour, passing, if necessary, right around the world and under the beds of the deepest oceans. The gigantic underground stations where these hurtling monsters paused for their freight had become places to marvel at for the essence of power and knowledge they flung at still puzzled Earthlings. Vaguely it was understood that Mayro's disintegrator machines had blasted away the toughest rocks into nothingness. A single ray-gun squad could accomplish in five minutes what old methods would have taken as many weeks to do.

Through the air, high atop the sky cities, floated the latest devices in air machinery—non-air airships. Amazing liners, equipped with vacuum copper globes, intake port engine rooms, revolving fan blades, fly wheels with gyroscopic action, and ports opened by rotating sleeves—tie entire craft gaining its lifting power by the buoyancy of a vacuum filled with a strangely multiplied power.

And lastly, across the Earth itself, shot queer glittering balls, deeply sunken within a curved railroad, and capable of a speed, at maximum, of something like six hundred miles an hour. Within these balls reposed the gyroscopic compartments, maintaining everything on a level keel while the outer shell revolved at a stupendous rate, hurling the vehicle with the speed of a super-bobsleigh down the appointed tracks.

Everywhere was speed unbelievable! Speed!

And across the sea moved ships controlled by distant radio, and others equipped with high-speed engines. The secret of atomic force was still one mystery that eluded even the brilliance of the visitors, though they were constantly working upon the problem.

The colossal alterations had, not unnaturally, caused the unemployment of a stagnant world to suddenly vanish. Every man and woman had an appointed place in the new scheme of things; everybody of a rational nature was entirely satisfied. Indeed, only a certain section of the extremely low classes, who had opposed the visitors ever since their arrival, gave any sign of trouble.

The band comprised, it appeared, some five thousand—a mere unit in the face of Earth's happy multimillions, but nevertheless, a force just unpleasant enough to cause Mayro much disgust that he had not a perfectly unanimous world.

"I would like to see this James Rawson, the leader of these discontented people," he confided one day to Crespin, when the whole Ruling Community had gathered together in their controlling edifice—the highest sky building in New York II.

"You see, Crespin, we start off on our lunar project tonight, and I do not wish to leave you here alone, to grapple with these lunatics. True, you have all the world at your back, but the opposers are without sense of justice or morality. They will sneak in by devious routes, destroy our power plants, lay the seed of discontent among the workers—maybe ruin all our work, without you being aware until it is too late."

"I think you worry needlessly over that," remarked Ramsey, chief mathematician to the Community. "Crespin can take care of himself—" Then, as though he were suddenly afraid of being asked questions, Ramsey turned away and stared out of the window upon the crazy panorama before him.

"I'll take a chance," Crespin replied grimly, his powerful chin setting firmly. "As for seeing Rawson face to face I don't think you'll ever manage that. He always keeps in the background. He has agents and spies, and a major-domo to do the talking when a personal contact becomes really necessary. Forget it, Mayro! It would take a supermind to disorganize this immensity of power and purpose. You have brought to our world an immeasurable degree of happiness and surety. And now you go to conquer another one and open it up; unearth its precious minerals; extend Earth's ramifications—split up into reborn life that very mausoleum in which you and your comrades were so long asleep."

Mayro nodded slowly. "And when it is done?" he asked thoughtfully. "I wonder what then? I have enjoyed this work—this progress; but when everything is finished and we have nothing more to do—" He stopped, then shrugged his mighty shoulders and smiled faintly. "I am delving too far ahead, my friends," he apologized, looking around. "We must get back to our project. Vane, is everything in readiness?"

The young astronomer nodded. "Everything. Fifty space ships, exactly to scale on your drawings, have been built, stored, and generally prepared for moon-colonization. They are waiting at the space grounds. Departure fixed for eight tonight."

"Excellent. Dr. Konsicks, are the men ready?"

"Yes—every man of them, all volunteers, with the exception of our own picked party. Of those present here, Vane, his wife, Ramsey, and of course you and your companions, will be going. You have the women ready for departure, too, Evelyn?"

"Yes," the girl nodded quickly. "They will be very necessary, too, to attend to matters at which men are only too futile."

"There may be danger—for women," said Mayro quietly.

"Women will risk danger if they love their men," Evelyn replied unflinchingly, and at that the giant scientist slowly inclined his white head.

"So be it, Evelyn. We will start to awaken the Earth's mausoleum—at eight tonight!"

* * * *

At eight o'clock, to the minute, the fifty space machines, composed of metal exactly similar to that of the visitors' ship—rendered possible by transmutation of elements which had finally produced the ray-emanating metal—took to the air, propelled through the atmosphere by the electric wave system—

Below, in the calm sunlight of the perfect summer evening, stretched a multitude of cheering people, bidding God-speed to those six men from space who had made heaven out of a world of incomparable chaos; bidding them luck on their daring project to give the Moon a second birth.

Then, in an amazingly brief stretch of time, the space ships, headed by Mayro's own machine—in which were he himself, his five colleagues, Konsicks, Vane and his wife—burst through the atmosphere's limits and into the void. Instantly the blazing radiations of the repulsive metal came into life, hurling the vessels away from the receding Earth at ever-mounting speed.

Acceleration was hardly noticeable, owing to the various devices with which the ships were equipped. Save for a slight pressure on top of the head nothing untoward was apparent.

The Moon, at the full, hung already clearer and larger in the flawless black of space, the stars and stardust passing dead to her edges, revealing only too clearly the absence of air. Behind, surrounded by the pink curtain of her atmosphere, was the crescent Earth, three quarters of her surface enveloped in somber green.

To the Earthlings, the view was one of surpassing wonder—the sheer beauty of celestial harmony took their breath away. They felt unable to tear themselves from the window, and indeed were quite irritated when the mature and cosmos-wise Mayro ordered them to rest, before the strain of constantly tolerating the slight acceleration pressure and blinding glare of the Moon upset their nerves.

So they retired to their bunks, in quarters specially prepared for them, slept very heavily, and awakened to find the vessel seemingly still. Through the portholes poured a harshly blazing white light, akin to arc lights trained on the whitest snow.

Puzzled, Vane and Evelyn entered the control room, to find Konsicks there with the visitors.

"We arrived about an hour ago," said Mayro quietly. "The glare you see is the sunshine on the crater walls. We have landed on the floor of Tycho. One half of our fleet is on the other side of the chasm—the chasm we created when emerging from the Moon's interior."

"We have arrived so soon?" Vane asked in astonishment.

"Why not? Have I not already told you of the speeds we can attain when necessary?"

"But there's no difference in gravitation—" Evelyn began.

"Purely because our floor gravitators are still at work," Mayro replied. "You will notice the difference when we get outside. I have communicated with the other ships by the short-wave radio system. They await our orders. The task must now begin."

"How?" Vane asked after a pause. "You have explained very little, Mayro."

"True; mainly because I thought that, back on Earth, should the news leak out, our enemies led by James Rawson might upset things. Here, I am free to speak.

"We have brought with us the wherewithal to build upon the Moon some twenty enormous towers, which will be placed in convenient positions amid the 14,600,000 square miles that comprise the Moon's surface. These towers will generate immense quantities of gas—oxygen and nitrogen being in the highest percentage. In time this gas will form into an atmosphere—that is the first thing we must do, and the density of the air we form here must, of course, be considerably more than that of Earth's, for here we have only one sixth of Earthly attraction. The Moon's gravitation will hold the atmosphere down, of course. All the work with the towers we shall accomplish in the space suits we have brought with us."

"It's going to be a big task," commented Konsicks reflectively.

"Beyond doubt, my friend—but worth it. Once the atmosphere has been created the biggest obstacle of all has been overcome— You are frowning, Konsicks! Why?"

The astronomer shrugged. "Somehow—I expect I'm an old fool!—I've got an idea that we're dabbling in things just a bit too big for us! Beating nature at her own game, so to speak. It doesn't do, Mayro! It never worked out yet!"

"A childish superstition, my dear friend," Mayro answered smilingly. "You will see! Once the atmosphere is made, the black sky of the Moon will banish and we shall have a blue one. The heat and cold will be tempered. We can create clouds to prevent the blazing sunlight— Yes, we can cultivate a perfect little world here. And now to business. We have no time to lose."

"What when night comes?" Vane sked.

"When that happens work will continue on the daylight side—the side always turned from the Earth. We shall follow the Sun."

Mayro turned aside and passed into the space-suit compartment. Twenty minutes later the entire party was outside on the rocky floor, gazing about them at the towering pinnacles of Tycho's crater through their smoked eyeglasses, glancing at times at the remarkable spectacle of the Sun and star-ridden sky and softly green "new" Earth.

Then attention swung to the remainder of the party, headed by Ramsey the mathematician, who were rapidly appearing from their various ships, on both sides of the chasm from which Mayro and his comrades had originally emerged. The others advanced slowly, their great boots weighing them down so that the lesser gravitation could play no capricious tricks.

By means of helmet phones, Mayro made the whole sequence of plans perfectly clear, and so there began, at the high noon of that month-long day, the most amazing task ever attempted by man—

* * * *

On Earth progress was watched through gigantic reflectors, and relayed by television to a waiting world. Months passed, and steadily there began to appear on the Moon's face the bristling spikes of towers at regular intervals. The various craters and dead seas of the Moon were littered with all manner of remarkable materials and super-engineering, devices. And, on the other side of the satellite, hidden from Earthly eyes, similar activity was taking place—for it proved to be entirely similar to the Earthward side, and not the harborer of some strange and fantastic civilization, as Vane had silently hoped.

Thrice trips were made to Earth for further supplies. A year passed—two years—three years. Then came a change: From the Earth, one September night in 1976, the Moon was seen to slowly change from an argent-faced globe into a satellite of writhing mists that boiled and swirled mysteriously over the entire face of that world. Every telescope and refractor was trained upon it. Across the Earth flashed the news. The Moon had an atmosphere!

And indeed it had. Through eight long months, ever since the towers had been completed, there had been pouring into the vacuum about the Moon a constant and enormous supply of oxygen and nitrogen, held to the Moon's surface when in small quantities by electromagnets, specially devised for the purpose, until finally there was enough to spread round the entire globe. Then, following natural law, the gases adjusted themselves so that when they reached a given height the density corresponded to the quantity of air above that height, this height acting as a weight pressing upon the air, and compressing its elastic substance until it had a density proportional to the pressure so produced.

So was the first stage reached. The pioneers of the Moon discarded their stuffy space suits and stepped out into a new world—a world with a sky of clouds, sheltered from the blazing rays of the sun. Work began with disintegrators and the leveling of the enormous mountain ranges and crater walls began.

It was grueling, relentless work, yet in the main the pioneers took pleasure in it. Vane and his wife set the example to other men and their wives, and as a consequence the soft-muscled astronomer and his sensitive wife changed into hard-bitten, tough adventurers, as strong as the rocks they destroyed, and as happy as the month-long day lasted.

Strange it was, too, how Earthlings found themselves working all through the month of daylight and sleeping a month of night. Conditions, the effect of time, the somewhat lighter air—having a pressure of ten pounds to the square inch against Earth's fourteen—aided speed and activity. The gravitation had at first been the biggest difficulty, but experience had overcome its tricks. It was the lesser gravitation, too, that made the destruction of mammoth mountain ranges remarkably simple, with a sixth of terrestrial resistance.

It was during this progress on the new world that Mayro made a radio announcement of paramount importance to the colonizers. He had discovered his long-sought-for secret of releasing atomic force! It appeared that experiments with a disintegrator had led him into the fields of copper-particle emanation, finally resulting in producing from a copper bar, some two inches long and half an inch thick, a source of stupendous power, which at will could be used as either a super-blasting machine or else inconceivably powerful magnetizing machine. The instant his discovery was made he went further and finally produced the Mayro Dredger—a prosaic name for a mighty discovery.

This apparatus, by a single frightful blast from its copper resources, completely destroyed an entire mountain range nearby. Not only that! The atomic force activity, reversed in action, drew the colossal boulders and stones in the debris to the encampment with tremendous speed, purely by magnetism, and deposited them there for building purposes—

So appeared another landmark in lunar history. From then on it was decided that the Dredger could do the work of thousands of men, and accordingly, a tower, larger than all the others, and composed of that remarkable radiation metal, was erected to a height of six hundred feet, with sheer unbreakable walls, possessing no visible doors, and supplied at the summit with a large-scale Dredger that could wield its power over an enormous area of the still hardly scratched lunar surface. Mayro was immensely enthusiastic over his discovery—so enthusiastic indeed that he failed to realize that in his discovery he had unwittingly laid the seed of discontent among Earth's strange and many-sided peoples. Where formerly men and women had toiled happily day by day, entirely thoughtless of any desire for anything else, they were now suddenly almost useless quantities—replaced by a flashing mammoth-force engine that leveled plains and removed mountains without visible effort. It even drew the heat of the sun to itself if left in action too long, and this fact caused the walls of the tower, being absorptive, to store up the heat and convert it into energy—hence, after a spell of considerable usage, the mighty tower would glow with radiations similar to those of the space ships, and, when the negative current was removed for any purpose, the structure became a literal blazing mass, emanating both the heat of the sun and that of its own natural radiation.

The colonists began to distrust the idea, wondered what was behind it all. So far everything had been all right, but now— Here and there unexpected dissenters sprang up and began to demand of the populace why they should strive and struggle on this hell satellite when Earth itself was perfectly comfortable?

Why shouldn't they go back to their native world and leave the maniacs from the cosmos to themselves? Who had started this fool idea to colonize a dead world, anyhow?

Dr. Konsicks saw the position clearly, and toward the end of one of the long lunar days, before retirement was to be made for the equally long night, he made the position understandable to Mayro and his comrades. Vane and Evelyn were present, too, listening in silent attention.

"Mayro, you don't seem even now to have thoroughly determined what idiots human beings can be at times!" Konsicks said grimly, his eyes bright behind his glasses. "The people here are thoroughly dissatisfied. For some reason not altogether clear, many have popped up like magic, men and women, and spread a desire for revolt. I understood all the men and women were sound, honorable people, but now—well, I begin to wonder."

"Do you mean you think there may be some men and women belonging to Rawson among them?" Vane asked quickly.

"Yes—just that," Konsicks assented gravely. "There was nothing to prevent Rawson's spies joining up as volunteers, of course—but I hardly thought they would do so. I thought they lacked both the nerve and the opportunity. It seems that I was wrong, and that they have seized the first chance to stir up trouble; when we were all working there was no sign of trouble. Plausible tongues can do a lot of damage, Mayro, particularly when backed by such a thing as your Dredger— I still feel no good will come out of this effort to colonize a dead world; just as I said before."

Mayro spread his hands. "I never for an instant thought Earthlings could be so basely ungrateful!" he said sorrowfully.

The doctor shrugged. "There is always a certain element like that. It can't be avoided, I'm afraid."

"Then what do you suggest I do? Destroy the Dredger?

"No; it is too valuable. We can only watch, and when the day comes again we will be on the alert. We'll consider giving the people back their work and using the Dredger for other purposes. It's the only way. Nobody can damage the Dredger, can they? If they did tamper with it, it could cause appalling damage in unexperienced hands—"

"You need not fear that, my friend," Mayro returned with utmost confidence. "That tower, as you know, is composed of indestructible metal, and has a secret door in the summit for egress only. The only way to enter the tower is via the hyper-space machine at the base camp, and nobody knows anything about that save ourselves, my five companions, and Ramsey, our mathematician. Frankly, I feel that you worry needlessly. Nothing will happen."

Konsicks nodded slowly. "Maybe you're right, Mayro, but you see I happen to know how strangely Earthlings behave at times. They will, if forced to it, destroy even their own mothers if they see an advantage in it. They are still—many of them—little better than the brute. However, I'm worrying no more now; I want some sleep. Coming, Vane? Evelyn?"

The two nodded and bidding the giant good night left the control chamber of the ship, which he and his companions, as a rule, continued to occupy.

V.

The night passed quietly enough, blanketed in by its new atmosphere, but toward its close strange movements became afoot among certain of the colonizers.

A party of six men moved with cautious footsteps across the rocky ground toward the silent base camp, as the main authoritative building was called. As was customary, a tireless colleague of Mayro's was on guard, watching over the various machinery upon which relied the advancement of the new-born moon's civilization.

"Right!" the leader of the party whispered presently, in a low voice. "Now's the time! We're lucky it isn't Mayro himself. Come on!"

With one accord they smashed through the immense window with a heavy boulder, and walked through, the opening—it being at ground level. The leader of the party leveled his rock disintegrator as Zanos, Mayro's closest friend, swung round in amazement.

"Make one move and you'll find yourself pure dust!" the leader growled. "O. K., boys—go to it. Tie him up."

The others made to follow the order, but Zanos suddenly sprang to life, his red eyes flaming. The machines were in danger, and that was all that concerned him. With one mighty bound of his enormous legs he strode across to the leader—then stopped as he saw the button on the disintegrator depress— There was no sound. Only a vivid flash of carmine light and gusts of scorching air. In one single instant of time, Zanos, seven foot eight of muscle and power, vanished utterly, reduced to the finest dust floating up to the single sub-radium lamp in the ceiling.

"You idiot, Jim!" breathed one of the party. "You shouldn't have done that! Mayro will tear the life out of you when he finds out!"

"He won't find out," the leader returned calmly. "Get busy with that hyperspace machine, Ramsey. You've spent long enough on its details to know how it works."

Ramsey, the mathematician, nodded slowly.

"Everything's worked out, Mr. Rawson," he answered quietly. "Here is the machine. The power switches on here." He pressed a button on the metal wall, and a series of rotating bars commenced to move up and down, at the same time emitting a bluish-white light upon a clear space beneath the machine's superstructure. "The number for the Dredger Tower is 4685. That will materialize you inside the tower. I've been with Mayro enough times, so I ought to know."

Rawson smiled with grim significance. "Great to have a guy like you, who's always by Mayro's side," he commented reflectively. "I don't like leaving you behind, all the same. You might spill something."

"If I'm not left behind Mayro will look for me," was Ramsey's cold answer. "Come on—let's get busy. You first, Morgan."

"I don't half like it—" Morgan began—but a fierce shove hurled him into the area of the blue light. The mathematician moved a massive pointer on the side of the instrument, swinging it round to the number 4685, then depressed the releasing button. In an instant Morgan vanished from view in a haze of swirling light.

"Seems all right." James Rawson commented presently. "Come on, Martin, get busy! And on second thought, Ramsey, since you're staying behind, you'd better wreck this hyperspace machine. That will stop any attack on us within the Tower if you choose to tell Mayro of our plans."

"You know how to get out of the Tower?" Ramsey asked indifferently.

"Sure! You told me all about the door at the top and the staircase—the metal that falls apart and can only be opened from inside. I know. So long as nobody gets in I'm not worried about getting out."

"Suppose I don't destroy this hyperspace machine?"

Rawson grinned unpleasantly. "You will, if you've any sense—else explain how it was that we got in the Tower. Remember you're the only outsider who knows how to work this darned thing—" He paused significantly. "You'll destroy it all right!"

With that he turned into the machine's area, and, one by one, the remaining men vanished from view. Ramsey, after the last man had gone stood in thoughtful silence for a space, then he shrugged his shoulders, pulled out his disintegrator, and leveled it at the exquisite machinery. Two carmine flashes and the machine was in irreparable ruins.

Ramsey passed it a final glance, nodded slowly, and then vanished into the slowly approaching lunar dawn outside, thinking mainly of the five men in the Dredger Tower, and wondering if they knew enough about the Dredger itself to control it from the detailed instructions he had given them—

* * * *

Norton Vane was literally shot out of slumber by the shaking of a violent hand. Opening his eyes sleepily he beheld the massive figure of Mayro himself by the side of the bunk, his usually calm, impassive face troubled, for perhaps the first time since his appearance in Earthly history.

"Quick! Quick! An astounding thing has happened!" he gasped out. "It threatens the entire solar system. I've awakened Konsicks. Get your wife and come to the control-room chamber on my ship right away!"

"All right," Vane replied drowsily. Fifteen minutes later, still half asleep, he and Evelyn reached the visitors' space ship, to find Mayro within, his grim-faced companions—only four of them this time—and a serious-eyed Dr. Konsicks.

"Well?" Vane asked interestedly. "What's the matter?"

"Do you notice anything peculiar about the daylight?" Mayro demanded presently.

Vane looked about him, then nodded in faint surprise. "Now that you mention it—yes. It seems sort of—well, a trifle reddish. Like a winter sun on Earth."

"Vane, Dr. Konsick's warning came too late," Mayro returned grimly. "During the night some unknown men have destroyed the hyperspace machine, and my dear friend Zanos, and have placed themselves in the Dredger Tower. Televised light waves have revealed that to me. They are using the atomic-force machine to their own advantage, but what it is I can't yet conceive. For some reason they are absorbing heat from the sun! And, with such appalling power at their command, the sun is fast *cooling!*"

"Good Lord!" Vane gasped blankly, and Evelyn uttered a little cry of dismay.

"You are sure you can't get into the Tower?" Konsicks asked keenly.

"Only too sure," Mayro answered, compressing his powerful lips. "The only way was by hyperspace, and as the machine for that is destroyed, it's useless. I was going to enter the Tower this morning, as is my usual custom, and I discovered the ruin I have mentioned. That means somebody among us knows who destroyed the hyperspace machine. It's one of us in here—or Ramsey, our mathematical expert— But never mind that for the moment. We will see what the infernal creatures are doing."

Turning, he hastily switched on an instrument by his side, already attuned to the Tower, and there appeared on the screen on the ship's wall a reproduction of the incidents taking place within the Tower itself, the televised system being capable, in the same manner as radio waves, of penetrating solids. Nor was a transmitter necessary. Trapping light waves from inside a solid was an elementary art to the visitors from the cosmos.

"What are they playing at?" demanded Vane in puzzlement, as he silently watched five men struggling desperately with switches and coils, and pointing ever and again to the mighty, glowing copper power plant which provided the power for the atomic force. Once, two of them rushed to the solid wall, beat impotently against it, and then fell back, to return with tottering footsteps to the power plant. It seemed that the very walls were shining.

"By heaven, don't you see who it is?" shouted Konsicks suddenly, pointing. "Look! It's the—"

"It's the man who knocked Evelyn down, and was afterward hammered by you, Mayro—when you arrived in Yuma Desert!" Vane rattled out, "Can he be Rawson, do you think? Or is he just an ally of his? Surely he's too unintelligent by himself—"

"Obviously he's unintelligent!" Mayro snapped out, consumed with fury. "Instead of using that atomic-force machinery for power, which probably was his original intention, he's got the reverse action and is using the magnetism effect. The result is that he is drawing the heat of the Sun constantly, in such vast quantities that before very long, unless we stop the maniac, the Sun itself will expire! The fool! The consummate idiot! Anybody with the vaguest knowledge of scientific machinery could control it. I wonder who put him up to this—"

"Mayro, may I speak to you?" asked a voice suddenly, and the giant swung round from his instrument to behold the slight figure of Ramsey in the control chamber.

"Well, Ramsey, what do you want?"

"Merely to tell you that I am mainly responsible for all this. Rawson's plans have gone wrong; he'll never escape that Tower alive— You see, I've been in Rawson's employ all along. Without me he was useless—he had neither brains nor science in his make-up. And, of course, being in close touch with you as well, it made his plans for your downfall singularly simple."

"What in the devil's name are you getting at?" demanded Vane savagely. "Come on, you lying scoundrel! Let's have it!" He shook the man with his powerful arms, until Mayro's compelling hand stopped him.

"Let me handle this, Vane— Now, Ramsey—the story! And quick!"

"There's not much to it," the mathematician answered slowly "I killed a man once—it was an accident—but Rawson heard of it and threatened to hand me to the law if I didn't help him with my mathematical knowledge. You had arrived on Earth, then, Mayro, and I was already in your employ. I saw no harm in doing what Rawson asked. He's coarse and uncouth; all the finer details have been my doing. As fast as I've learned anything I've passed it on to Rawson—and it was I who started the rebellion idea on the Moon here; I stirred up trouble with the people, using Rawson's agents for the purpose. Of course, it was easy for him to get to the Moon here by a simple disguise; I took care of the details.

"Rawson hates you, Mayro—has hated you ever since that day in the desert when you broke his jaw. His only desire ever since has been to destroy you and your works, and, being something of a power in the criminal world of Earth, he's done quite well, with me to help him. His chance here came when you discovered your Dredger. He decided, with the information I'd given him, to use the Dredger as a force machine and radiate your ship and all your works out of existence—then allow Earthlings to return to Earth. Nothing more than that. Not world power, or anything so fantastic. Purely a blind hatred for you. With your destruction and the return of everybody to Earth, he would have been satisfied. To destroy Earthlings' faith in you was in the first move; to destroy you the second, and to return to Earth the third."

"And you know what has happened?" Mayro asked in a measured, relentless voice.

"Yes." Ramsey considered for a moment; then lightly, "It's rather a pity, really."

"Pity!" Vane exploded furiously. "Why, you damnable, callous—"

"With their clumsy blunderings they have switched on magnetic force instead of the disruptive," interposed Mayro, in the same merciless voice. "They can't stop the machinery, and neither can anybody else! They're trapped in the building and don't know the way out."

"I explained it to them," Ramsey replied calmly. "If they can't find it, it's their own fault." He glanced at the screen and raised his eyebrows. "Hm-m-m, they do seem to be having slight difficulty, don't they?"

All five men were on the floor now, only moving occasionally. The walls were gleaming even brighter, and the copper in the power plant shone brilliant green.

"The door in that Tower opens, as you know, Ramsey, by sound vibration," Mayro remarked grimly. "Did you know when you sent them there that they couldn't possibly duplicate those sounds without the instruments for the purpose? Such as we carry?"

"I wonder if I did?" the mathematician asked enigmatically. "I do know, though, that I expected them to be successful and not make such idiots of themselves. You see, I expected them to switch on the power for disruptive force, but before it could do any damage here the recoiling power alone would have crushed the life out of them. They couldn't find the way out without the sound machine for opening the door— Dear me—really a bad mistake! They managed to switch on the power all right—but got magnetism by mistake— My dream of dispatching Rawson in a spectacular way has been shattered, indeed."

"You planned their destruction quite skillfully," remarked Mayro presently, his voice still with that inflexible intonation in its depths, "but at heart, Ramsey, you are as big a devil as they. All my work here—everything—has been ruined. That is bad enough, but by all the gods I can never forget that your meddling resulted in the death of my beloved comrade, Zanos. You have a price to pay, Ramsey."

The mathematician started at that and shot a glance of dismay at the relentless red eyes fixed upon him. His nonchalant manner vanished in a trice.

"You don't mean you would kill me?" he gasped out. "I didn't kill Zanos! I was all against it!"

"He was killed as the result of your underhand methods, and that suffices," Mayro replied coldly. "I am sorry—but you have reason to know that we are a just but unsentimental people. Goodbye, friend Ramsey."

The mathematician swung round at that and made desperately for the door—but before he had got halfway a carmine beam followed him. Came one horrible shout, then a thin blue smoke was drifting through the control-room door into the red sunlight outside—Ramsey, mathematician and traitor to a mighty cause, had ceased to be.

Mayro slipped his instrument back in his belt and looked round for a space at the silent, faintly horrified faces of the Earthlings. Then with a shrug he looked back at the screen on the wall.

"The heat is killing them," he remarked presently. "As time passes the heat will get worse. Every vestige of heat in the Sun is being drawn relentlessly by that power plant, passing into the absorptive, radio-active walls of the Tower itself. The end is inevitable—" He stopped and turned. "We have no alternative, my friends, but to leave as quickly as possible! We must leave the moon and return to Earth; warn Earth's peoples what is happening. They must take all precautions for a period of terrible cold owing to the withdrawal of the sun's heat. In two weeks, and that is the life of the copper in the plant, the sun will be burned out, every vestige of its heat energy trapped within that Tower—to what end we cannot even guess, as yet."

"But surely we can get in the Tower—do *something?*" Vane demanded desperately; but Mayro shook his massive head.

"No, friend Vane. I know from experience that that Tower is impregnable. You were right, Konsicks. To try and colonize this world was going against the law of nature—we have failed! Once back on Earth we must turn our activities to determining how to create—if possible—another sun. Come, Konsicks, we must raise the alarm."

Once the situation was made clear to the astonished Earthlings, the exodus from the moon began at breakneck speed. The power tower was already commencing to glow on the outside and emitted an appalling, scorching heat over a distance of five miles. Once or twice Vane tried to guess at what would ultimately happen, but without success. The only conclusion he could arrive at was that the Tower would finally burst asunder—

Yet, how could this be? The metal was indestructible, and incapable of bursting or melting. Its sole purpose was that of storing and retaining energy, and such a mass as the power tower was capable of storing even the entire energy of Sirius itself without coming to any harm, let alone the tiny sun of the Earthly solar system.

Vane gave up the problem finally, and five hours later the entire fleet of pioneers, disgruntled at failure, were in space heading toward Earth, leaving behind them that still-operative copper plant, and the five dead men beside it who had so successfully ruined the attempt to colonize Earth's satellite, to meet their deaths in that very selfish endeavor. Poetic justice—but certainly no consolation—

Back on Earth the news was publicly broadcast, of course, from the controlling edifice in the sky which Mayro promptly took over on his return. Orders were given for the immediate preparation of heat machines in every available quarter of the Earth to stave off the appalling cold and darkness that was to come.

And so, through fourteen frenzied days, mankind toiled and struggled in a fast-waning daylight and pitch-dark nights to erect all manner of devious heat machines, from ordinary steam radiators to electric and sub-radium arcs. Mayro, tireless, brooded over all this activity with knitted brows, and, on the thirteenth evening, watched a red, almost extinct sun sinking below the western horizon, the amazing sky city etched out in a silhouette of ink before it. Of the moon there was no sign, of course, owing to the sun's failure to provide light. The only trace of the satellite that remained was a faint radioactive glow in the heavens, occasioned by the power tower itself.

"There we see the last of the sun," Mayro commented grimly. "For thirteen days the lunar power plant has been drawing its heat energy at an inconceivable speed, and by tomorrow morning—and there will be no daylight!—our Sun will be a dead star. Burned out—as though there had been some colossal short circuit in the void! I cannot even now understand why all that energy doesn't react in some way—its stupendous power and force. Let me think— Something has got to be done to provide Earth with light and heat again. Leave me, Vane—you, too, Konsicks. I must think this out."

"Very well," answered Konsicks, and the two left the meditative Mayro to grapple with the gigantic problem alone and—

It was in the light of an arc lamp that he reappeared to Vane, Evelyn and Konsicks, the three of them slumped on chairs in an anteroom, fast asleep. Quietly he woke them.

"I have it," he said very gravely. "The cause and the cure! It is now high noon, but the sun has not appeared; its extinguishment is complete. But, that energy has all gone into the walls of the power tower on the Moon. Knowing the peculiarities of that metal, I realize that the reason for the energy being dormant is because there is no friction to cause it to be released. It is simply there—a tremendous mass of energy, waiting—for friction."

"Friction?" repeated Konsicks, sitting up.

"Yes. Don't you understand, knowing metal, that that energy is at a uniform level? It has passed into the power plant, into the absorptive walls of the power tower, into the very ground of the moon itself. Atomic force, my friends, is mingled with it, but, as our experiments have proved, atomic force cannot be liberated without friction to commence the disintegration. Friction—that molecular disruption action—commences the entire process which afterwards goes on indefinitely."

"Yes, but what—" Vane began.

"Just this, friend Vane. The Earth shall have another sun! It has lost the energy of one, but that energy has passed into another body—the Moon. Friction will be generated on the Moon, strong enough to start the relatively infinitesimal spark that will set atomic force spreading all over the moon's surface. You understand? A hurtling flight into the very midst of the power tower itself, creating a band of fire through the atmosphere we have created—frozen now, I expect—and then— Fire! *Atomic* fire! Which will instantly kindle itself and become liberated energy. Flame and heat will finally turn the moon into a blazing sun, with an indefinite life of tens of thousands of years, until every atom and molecule has been exploded and destroyed."

"But, Mayro, who on Earth is going to do such a thing?" Evelyn asked wonderingly. "To do that will mean complete annihilation!"

Mayro shrugged, a strange light in his red eyes. "In the beginning, it was my friends and I that started all this trouble," he said slowly. "We have consulted each other, and we are agreed that we have no real place on Earth. Through us, indirectly, the sun has been burned out; it is only just that it be us who restore it. You have gained something from the cities and inventions we have given you, perhaps, but now our work is indeed at an end. You remember I once said I wondered what would happen when our work was ended. Now you know. My comrades and I are of one mind in that the moon shall again be our mausoleum—perhaps more than that. A colossal crematorium, in which we shall instantly perish. What does it matter? Our work is ended, and on Earth we are no longer needed—or probably even wanted. Better release our minds from these cumbersome bodies—"

"So, for the sake of saving a world you are prepared to sacrifice yourselves?" Konsicks asked in a low voice, after a long pause. "After the benefits you have bestowed, too! We cannot allow you to do it, Mayro! We'd never forgive ourselves."

"My dear friend, be reasonable!" Mayro replied. "Earthlings today are facing a world which is dark and sunless. True, they can exist by the various heating devices that have been erected, for quite some little time—but there is bound to be a quick ending to it all. Earth will freeze—the atmosphere will solidify. No man-made heating devices can take the place of the all-powerful sun. Science is not so far ahead as that."

"But, Mayro, cannot a projectile be fired at the Moon from here?" Evelyn asked.

"How, dear lady?" the giant inquired gravely. "Just how? A projectile could never be satisfactorily guided through 240,000 miles of space to impinge dead on that power tower. Besides, the moon's surface is dark owing to the sun's failure. Not until we get really close to it, near enough to see the radiations of the power tower, can we find the correct vantage point. No, a personally driven space ship is the only way. Please do not worry about us, my friends," he went on earnestly. "My companions and I are not afraid of death; it is purely a new scientific experience— We depart in an hour."

And with that Mayro thoughtfully left the chamber, leaving the Earthlings gazing after him in silent admiration. That such nobility of purpose could ever have come out of the cosmos was something new to them, and inwardly they reproached themselves for ever once having dared to think that the visitors might be hostile.

Hostile! Where was there an Earthling who would make such a sacrifice for another world?

* * * *

By the special request of Mayro the population of New York II was not informed of his decision. There was no need for Earthlings to leave their heated fortresses in order to demonstrate praise and good will. Such was the matter-of-fact way in which Mayro and his comrades surveyed the matter. And indeed they certainly did not appear at all perturbed at the merciless task they had allotted to themselves.

Konsicks, Vane and Evelyn, wrapped to the ears in furs, were the only ones who accompanied the visitors through the dark sunless silences of the sky city's ground levels to the space grounds. The air was relentlessly cold; the thermometers revealed 20-below freezing, and falling steadily every minute. It came to the Earthlings in a passing thought how futile were all the efforts of man compared to those of celestial power—

Quietly, Mayro singled out his own space ship and stood aside for his companions to enter the warm interior. Lights came up in the control chamber. For a moment he stood in the manhole aperture, silhouetted against the light from within.

"Goodbye, my friends," he said gravely. "It has been an interesting period, and we have left you a world worth having. You are hundreds of years ahead of what you would have been normally. As Konsicks once said—it is a mistake to try and colonize a world which the fates have deemed extinct. In approximately eight hours, for we shall waste no time, the dead Moon will kindle into life as we strike the control tower. You will have a very near sun, but on account of its infinitely smaller size compared to the dead sun you should experience no discomfort. Farewell my friends."

"Goodbye, Mayro," replied the three, almost in one voice, and Vane cursed himself for a sentimental idiot when he found his eyes were suddenly, strangely wet. He turned to find Evelyn openly and unashamedly crying.

The spaceship door closed. Came a short interval in which the silence seemed more oppressive—then with utter noiselessness the ship suddenly lifted from the ground and shot into the blackness. A faint streak from its electrical radiations, mounting ever higher—then it was gone. Three Earthlings were left, staring into the star-sprinkled vault above.

For quite a time they remained thus, then, the biting cold creeping into their bones, they turned and walked slowly back to the controlling edifice, operated the immense elevator that took them to the summit, and returned to the warmth and light of the main chamber.

Almost without a word they seated themselves at the immense window, switching off the light that they might have a better view.

"Eight hours," murmured Konsicks presently, glancing at his watch. "That means that at approximately eight o'clock tonight we shall see the moon—entirely invisible at first, of course—kindled into life, if the gallant Mayro and his comrades are fully successful. If not—Earth is doomed."

Vane and his wife said nothing. They sat huddled together, staring over the dark and slowly freezing immensity outside, wondering how other Earthlings were faring in the deadening cold—or else pondering upon the mind motivating the selfless being known as Mayro somewhere in the depths of space, deliberately driving a space ship to destruction and incontinent doom to himself and companions—

The hours passed. The darkness remained unmitigated. The stars shifted slightly with the passage of hours. It was strange to notice the absence of the planets, Mars, Venus and Jupiter. Owing to the sun's failure these worlds, too, must have suddenly experienced sudden and complete iciness—nor would the kindling of the moon be of any use to them, being both too small and too distant. The life of Mars and Venus, if any, had been snuffed out for eternity. The whole cosmic order of things had changed unbelievably—all because one man, the deceased James Rawson, had nursed a grievance!

The three partook of perfunctory meals and then returned to the window to watch. Twice during the 'day' they received messages from Crespin, who was with his immediate officials in the astronomical edifice seven miles away. Only to him did Konsicks reveal the visitors' sacrifice. Then, waiting again. Until at length the time began to draw to a close. It was almost 8 p.m.—

In their minds' eye the three could picture what was happening. And their imagination was very close to actual truth.

Sweeping, even at that moment, down toward the frozen desolations of the moon, in which was imprisoned the inactive energy of the Sun and unprogressive atomic force, was Mayro's space ship. An omnipotent observer might have seen it for an instant as a blazing silver streak, hurtling through the moon's now semi-frozen air with undiminished speed. During the journey through space it had reached a pace of approximately 98,000 miles *a* second—half that of light; a speed which had been gradually attained, taking eight hours in all to accomplish—but now, as Mayro swung round the ship's nose toward the faintly glowing mass of the silent power tower, he made no effort to decelerate. His jaw merely set a little tighter; his comrades waited patiently at their posts.

Faster—faster— The power tower's mass hurtled upward with inconceivable speed until—

The space ship crashed dead in the center! In an instant it was reduced to blazing flame by the appalling collision. In one split second Mayro and his companions were literally rubbed out—became cosmic dust. A mighty mass of boiling, livid green and white flames spewed outward from the moon's surface, expanding such enormous energy and heat that in another second the moon's surface itself caught fire. Without a second's pause the atmosphere followed suit, the atomic energy releasing itself, which in turn released the stored-up energies that had been drawn from the sun. As though some stupendous match had been applied to an inexhaustible supply of gas.

Mightier and mightier became the conflagration—a mixture of atomic and solar fire. The energy of the moon's mass itself began presently to disrupt and flame—and would continue to do so through tens of thousands of years until at length every scrap of atomic power had been destroyed—

* * * *

On Earth, Vane, Evelyn and Konsicks started into life as they suddenly beheld low down on the eastern horizon, where the moon should have been rising, a mass of green and white flame. Crespin and his men saw it also at the same instant, and became stricken with amazement at the sight.

Climbing gradually into the heavens, the Earth turned on her axis and the moon also shifted its position, came that flaring ball, already a mass of searing flame, pouring heat down on the frozen Earth. The sky began to take on blueness.

"He made it!" yelled Vane, jumping up and down. "Lord bless Mayro! He did it!"

"Don't go outside until things warm up a bit," counseled Konsicks, as mature as ever, his thick glasses gleaming in the light.

So, gradually, the entire mass of the moon became incandescent, became a literal sun at a distance, on an average, of 240,000 miles. As she swung nearer there came a summer season, and as she moved away, came a winter. Later, experience proved this fact.

Within a week Earthlings emerged into the open to take stock of their surroundings. Save for extreme cloudbursts when the warmth had returned, and three tidal waves caused by the cosmic shiftings, Earth was little the worse off—and from then onward the weather-controlling machines kept the climate normal the world over.

The only changes that would be noticeable would be in years to come, for, as the moon's bulk was transformed slowly into pure gas, her mass would consequently lessen until she became a globe of heat. This would cause the Earth to shift its position owing to the altered gravitational pull, but so slight would be the movement, and so gradual its accomplishment, scientists did not consider the matter of vital concern.

At first difficulties were experienced by sunrise being varied in its arrivals, but at length an arbitrarily fixed sunrise and sunset of twenty minutes later each time was arrived at, and Earthlings slowly adapted themselves to the change, The tides too, underwent several changes owing to the gravitational alterations, and new coast lines were made while others disappeared—

The visitors from the cosmos had come—and gone. They had left behind them a world of enormous progress and speed, wherein the vast majority was happy and contented. A world of curious sky cities, hurtling conveyances, and a perfect understanding of space travel. A Sun had been destroyed, and another reborn—and many were the times that Vane and his wife would glance up at the flaming mass, or study it from the Californian observatory, left untouched at Konsicks' request, and think of the giants who had come from within that ice-bound mausoleum, to transform it finally into their celestial funeral pyre.

METAMORPHOSIS

With fierce, argumentative intensity the two men paced about Professor Draycott's expansive Californian estate. Draycott himself, fifty years of age and world renowned as a physicist, only paused occasionally to thump home some point with fist and hand, then waited whilst Dr. Andrews, his closest friend and partner, gave his opinion.

"I tell you, man, that the thing's dangerous!" Andrews declared at last, coming to an emphatic standstill. "Do you realize for one moment what we are proposing doing? Matter out of energy! I never thought before of the chance we're taking."

Draycott shrugged; his seamed face was confident enough.

"Listen, Andrews," he said quietly, "you've got to admit that matter and energy are pretty much of a puzzle, anyhow. I don't need to tell you that the universe is sparsely filled with matter. Here and there this matter formation is visible in the form of planets, human beings, plants, and so forth. I believe that once, and only once, there was an accident in space, an accident whereby a range of radiations far shorter even than those of cosmic rays—probably a wave of about one thirty-second of a million millionth of a centimeter—struck a mass of energy in space.

"I say 'mass' quite figuratively, mind you. That resulted in fusion, and matter was just born. I believe, too, that, in the early stages, matter was alive and possessed of mentality, of an order we cannot understand. Later it formed into an outwardly expansive matter and finally exploded, producing the galaxies and scattered matter seas that we know as the expanding universe of today. When that explosion happened, certain of the radiations released reacted on the then inanimate carbohydrates of Earth and produced yet another form of life, which ultimately evolved into human beings.

"The real life that had formerly existed—some electrical form, no doubt—lost potency and became inanimate. Today we know that unintelligent life as electricity. Nothing more. I believe that electricity is the *real* life of the universe. We are merely accidents, offshoots of what was intended to be an infinitely greater power."

"I know all that," Andrews said.

"Maybe you do; but since you're feeling uncertain, it's perhaps as well to refresh your memory. Our calculations have proven that only a wave length of the order already mentioned could possibly change free energy into solid matter. I think, if we can do it, that we would find a form of matter exactly reproducing the one that originally formed the closely packed core that has now become the scattered, exploding mass of the universe."

"I still think we're taking too big a risk," Andrews muttered. "We're doing something that hasn't been done since time began, and, frankly, I don't like the thought of it."

"My dear chap, one would think this was the first time you'd weighed the experiment up. You know as well as I do that our matrix will just stand the temperature we shall need—and only just, if our calculations are right, since it will mean involving a temperature of some two thousand billion degrees. We shall use copper for the experiment, since it gives its energy freely, then, when it is finally annihilated into energy, it will be bombarded, before dissipation is possible, by ultra-short cosmic-ray wave lengths, identical to those which we believe brought the matter part of our universe into being. Of course it will be risky. What experiment isn't? But if it succeeds, think what we have accomplished! We shall not only have annihilated inanimate matter but will have changed it into another form of matter altogether. Duplicated creation, in fact!"

"That's what is worrying me," Andrews responded dubiously. "I'm a scientist, yes. But I'm beginning to feel chary at trying to beat Nature at her own game."

Draycott sniffed. "Fine talk after years of assembling equipment, after endless hours of computation, struggle, and designing. Now we come to the crucial point your nerve is failing you. We have everything down to the last figure, even how to alter the wave lengths of inflowing cosmic rays to the required length we need. Why, you yourself invented that device, perhaps the smartest thing you ever did.

"First we draw the cosmic waves by electromagnetic devices, then pass them on to the transformer chamber. There they are subjected to perpetually varying electrical fields, generating tens of thousands of volts, which change the radiations ultimately to what we want. Thence they pass, the instant they are needed, to our matrix. And then, Andrews, you dare to flinch!"

Andrews shrugged. "Maybe I'm a fool," he admitted. "Suppose, though, there is a violent explosion that blasts not only us, but everything on Earth, right out of being?"

Draycott smiled with a certain fatalism. "If there is, we shan't need to worry over it, shall we? On the other hand, we may meet with success. I'm quite convinced that in electricity, in the terrible force of atomic energy, in the weaker and destructive wanderings of thunderstorms, in the strange power begotten of friction, there is a *something*—a something lying dormant that our experiment may bring to life. The things we shall tamper with will involve electricity of the nth degree, and if our conclusions on the beginning of the universe are correct, we are but the lowliest form of life, permitted supremacy only because our masters are asleep."

He paused and glanced toward the sunset.

"Getting chilly," he said abruptly. "Besides, it's time for dinner. Come."

* * * *

The two scientists ate dinner with the same enthusiasm as they had always done. It was an agreement between them that at mealtimes they shelved all things scientific. But immediately it was over they retired to the laboratory and became men of action once more.

"Tonight!" breathed Draycott, gazing round at the bulky apparatus filling the half-mile expanse. "The night we've waited for all these years, Andrews! When we are to put all our treasured ideals and beliefs to the vital test! Smile, man—smile! It's a supreme moment. Even if it is to mean our deaths, we can only die once. Why not in so glorious a cause?"

The stoop-shouldered Andrews shrugged and looked doubtfully at the cold and silent electric furnace in the center of the laboratory.

"All right, let's go," he said simply, and with that proceeded to go through the actions he had performed in pantomime for months previous. This experiment was to be no mere haphazard stunt, no groping effort to wrest an impossible secret, but a skilled and practiced endeavor backed by unswerving knowledge and countless rehearsals.

Whilst Draycott placed the copper block, perhaps three inches square, in the matrix, and enclosed it with the specially designed pressure plates and sheathing, Andrews checked over his cosmic-ray machinery. In appearance it somewhat resembled a high-powered telescope, save that it was much more solidly built. Its far end poked inquisitively into the clear night sky through the opened roof. From long experiment both men knew the constant prevalence of cosmic rays by day and night, but only they had managed to devise the necessary means to snare them.

At last everything was in order. The cosmic-ray transformer chamber was in position, completely linked to the furnace, ready for the vital moment. Draycott threw in the switches, then he and Andrews stood in silence and slipped tinted goggles into position over their eyes as a safeguard. Andrews bit his lip and stared fixedly at the apparatus; Draycott watched the specially designed furnace fascinatedly, swiveling his eyes only occasionally to the readings on the heat and pressure gauges.

Rapidly the air began to become hot and stifling. The two discarded their coats and collars, and stood looking very unscientific in their shirt sleeves. Higher and higher rose the temperature.

How long they waited they had no idea; they were too interested in their task. It was impossible to judge what was happening inside the furnace; they could only call on their scientific imaginations to picture the disruption of matter. In that there was nothing so very abnormal. Scientists had done this before, but perhaps not so thoroughly. It was the conjecture of the latter part of the experiment that gripped them.

Dead to the second, timed absolutely by the various meters, Draycott swung around to his switchboard again and proceeded to shift the vital controls. The cosmic-ray apparatus moved automatically into position. Andrews leaped to it, flung in the switches of the transformer chamber. The electromagnetic attractors glowed white hot. Then he looked up tensely, his eyes on the dials—turned and nodded a glistening face.

Immediately Draycott slammed in the master switch. At the identical second the composition of the copper within the furnace, passed into the pure-energy state, but, also, at that same, identical second there hurtled upon it the terrific power of cosmic rays, focused into a single devastating convergence and shortened to one thirty-second of a million millionth of a centimeter.

The two men never beheld what happened after that. It seemed that the universe suddenly opened like a yawning, flaming abyss. They were dropped into the blazing maw of a terrific incandescence, all vestiges of life instantly blasted out of them.

Southern California heaved and shook in its entirety. For an area of a hundred miles around the Draycott estate the landscape rose and fell like a carpet with the wind beneath it, razing buildings to the ground in clouds of choking dust, burying the hapless inmates. The scientist's own residence simply spewed upward into the sky in a smashing mass of masonry, blasted outward *en bloc* by the violence of an incredibly powerful explosion.

Where the residence and grounds had stood there was naught but a two-mile-wide crater. But in the center of that crater, glowing as yet with fiendish brilliance and unimaginable heat, lay a heavy, rocklike piece of matter, the most remarkable matter ever known on Earth.

And with the passing of the hours, whilst people throughout the world, and in America in particular, rushed frantically to and fro trying to discover what had taken place, whilst meteorologists pored unbelieving over zigzagged seismograph charts, the metal began to cool. But, even so, there were none who yet dared to approach within ten miles of it, none whose eyes dared to look, even from the air, upon its blinding grandeur.

II.

It was a week later before the metal cooled, and one of the first on the scene was Gordon Wood, a New Yorker, scientific administrator for the United States. This lean, industrious man with the clipped mustache and penetrating gray eyes, handled the problem with true scientific energy and regard for caution.

He knew that the meteorite, as it was then popularly supposed to be, might be extremely dangerous; indeed, in view of the terrific explosion it had caused, it was more than likely. He immediately had the scene of activity roped off, then waited whilst special freight cranes were sent across the continent from the research institute in New York City, whither the metal was finally conveyed in the grip of massive steel clamps, always kept well away from the possibility of human touch.

Since the substance was considered definitely in the meteorite class it was not altogether Wood's fault that he did not at first personally examine it. It was conveyed, when thoroughly cooled, for examination by the meteorite research department.

A young expert by the name of Stanley was assigned to conduct the investigation, but when, not two hours afterward, Wood was summoned and found only a pool of water where Stanley should have been, he began to suspect there was something very radically wrong. Questioning of various assistants revealed that Stanley had decided on examining the stuff on his own. He had cried out. Others had rushed in to find—a pool of water!

It was certainly no meteorite that could behave in so deadly a fashion. Wood had it transferred by special apparatus to his own quarters and there, in company with his colleague, Nick Easton, began a specialized and careful study.

"It's darned funny stuff, Nick," he commented, after a half-hour examination from a respectful distance by means of binocular apparatus. "You've seen the tests for yourself. The substance doesn't fit into anything in the periodic table. It's an extremely heavy, unknown metal, highly electrical, and deadly to human life if you get too near it. Remember poor Stanley's fate! He must have fingered it."

Nick Easton rubbed a puzzled hand through his blond hair, eyed the ill-formed dirty-gray substance doubtfully.

"I can't figure out what happened to him," he muttered, frowning. "There was only a pool of water; the body had gone— flesh, bones, blood, and all the lot. What do you make of it?"

Wood pondered an interval, then looked at his colleague grimly.

"I'll tell you," he answered slowly. "The whole thing can be judged somewhat by its own weight. You see, before Stanley examined it, this substance according to our recordings, was four pounds lighter and two square inches less than it is now. That apparently proves that it somehow absorbed all the electricity in poor Stanley's body and turned it to its own uses. Blasted him utterly out of being and left only water, the basic element of his constitution. Probably that would have gone, too, had we left the metal there long enough. Fortunately, we were called in before, that occurred, and also before anybody else got involved. At least, we have that to be thankful for."

"Then—then you mean that the stuff is definitely electrical?"

"What else?" Wood relapsed into silence again, stroking his chin. "I can't just believe that this thing *is* a meteorite," he said at last.

"Normally, a meteorite ought to be just—well, anything. Anything metallic, that is, but certainly not at all dangerous. This stuff, if you get too near, is like grabbing a live wire— in fact, worse, because it produces instant vaporization. That points to something in an energy form that we never heard of before. Hm-m-m—a *new* energy, eh?" He turned aside, struck with a sudden thought, and pulled down an immense filing register from the shelf behind him.

With a frown in his face, he went through the sheets and finally fixed an acid-stained finger on one particular entry.

"May, 1935!" Gordon Wood exclaimed suddenly, and Nick peered over his shoulder. "That was just over three years ago. Professor Sampson Draycott and Dr. Charles Andrews, both of them physicists, filed papers here relating to a system of creating matter out of energy. At that time they wanted financial backing, but the board refused to allow it on the grounds that the theory was too vague and impractical. Now I just wonder—"

"Wonder what?"

"Well, Draycott lived in California. This metal was found on approximately the very site where his home had once been. It seems to me too much of a coincidence. I am wondering if this metal had anything to do with the experiment—if he tried it privately and, by some incredible fluke, succeeded. If so—" Wood's eyes began to brighten. He snapped the register shut. "If so, Nick, we've something here that doesn't fit into anything Earthly! It may be capable of anything. Matter born of energy never happened except by natural processes, such as when the universe was born. Damn it! If only one could approach the stuff!" He looked at it longingly, in the grip of the steel-clawed machine.

He and Nick both fell silent, thinking, and as they did so the quiet of the laboratory was disturbed by a peculiar, unexpected sound. It was the very faintest hissing noise, like steam rising out of a kettle. Wood aroused himself as it continued and looked round in puzzlement. Then, finally, his eyes settled on the metal as the cause.

"Good heavens!" he exclaimed, wide-eyed, then started violently as the lump suddenly began to visibly expand, accruing substance to itself like some metallic protoplasm. Nor were the steel clamps that held it of any further use. It burst them and fell heavily to the floor, continuing to enlarge. Then, as suddenly as it had commenced, it stopped once more. The hissing note ceased.

"Got it!" Nick exclaimed, snapping his fingers. "I'll bet it's the battery in the clamper itself! The metal's taken the juice out of it. Try it. I'll wager I'm right."

Wood nodded, and they both sidled round the now quiescent metal at a distance. Wood picked up a voltmeter and quickly placed its contacts across the battery terminals of the machine. Not the slightest kick was registered.

"Flat as a pancake!" he cried amazedly. "You were right, Nick. The darn thing eats electricity all right and grows thereby. We'll have to move it to a safe place."

"Such as?

"Down in the cellars under this building, where we keep the dry goods. It'll be safe enough there from electricity. Clear the building of people. I'll use the automatic crane. Get busy!"

Nick promptly departed.

It took Wood nearly an hour to again clamp that dangerous piece of metal, and when at last he did succeed it was transported down the slanting slide to the cellars and there left to lie in darkness until those above could figure out a new way of dealing with it.

Certainly it was safe enough in the cellar from all normal disturbances. Had it possessed the power of motivation it would probably have climbed through the grating that led to the busy main street outside. Since it did not, it lay in silence, radiating a peculiar bluish glow that caused concern to come to the faces of those scientists who looked at it from time to time from the top of the cellar slide.

* * * *

By nine o'clock that night the institute was quiet and silent. Old Meadows, the veteran caretaker, wandered with his electric torch through the immense reaches of the place, taking his usual course through the ghostly aisles lined with gleaming bottles and impedimenta.

For an hour he pursued his usual limping course from ground floor to tenth and down again, then, purely in the line of duty, descended into the cellar. Having received no warning of what lay there—indeed, Wood had never even thought the old man was so thorough in his nocturnal prowlings—he was not unnaturally puzzled by the strangely glowing substance down there in the gloom. Thoughts of thieves passed through his unimaginative mind.

Steadily, he limped down the long stone slope, torch clutched in a gnarled hand, and came presently within a foot of the metal. He began to laugh at his fears; then the laugh froze on his lips. Strange sensations were creeping over him. He took a hasty step backward.

A searing pain shot throughout his body, flamed every nerve with unbearable anguish, crushed his mentality into the numbing darkness of eternity. His body pitched to the floor as though struck with a trip hammer, and hardly had it done so before it began to deliquesce, vaporized, and completely vanished. The remaining pool of water went last, evaporated into nothing. The outflung torch, still lighted, suddenly expired, the power of its small battery consumed.

For a while after that nothing happened; the strange electrical protoplasm was sufficiently gorged. Its odd hissing rose on the silence and presently ceased. Then again it rose into activity. The acquisition of the electricity from the watchman, together with the slight percentage from the torch battery, had given it just the power necessary to expand its size and extend its influence over a wider radius.

There were many in the main street outside who swore to the fact that at about ten fifteen, twisting streamers of writhing electricity leaped from the cellar gratings of the research institute, and finally fastened themselves in colossal festoons to the street-car overhead wires.

In one tremendous surge the astounding substance absorbed all the power from the wires, so swiftly, so devastatingly, that its substance could not keep pace with the stimulus provided. Consequently, it burst, and the entire research institute hurtled upward and outward from the force of a gigantic explosion.

The shock was felt all over New York. Windows smashed; streets were torn up, and, simultaneously, all street cars stopped dead. Frantic engineers in the power houses raced to and fro looking for a technical fault. But, to their infinite amazement, they found nothing was visibly wrong! The generators and dynamos were functioning as smoothly and flawlessly as they had always done.

Fire engines, hastily summoned, raced to the blazing site of the research institute and got to work. A vast crowd turned out to see the blaze, swarming round the isolated, immovable street cars in a pushing, excited mob.

Within the private laboratory of Gordon Wood's home the telephone jangled noisily. Impatiently, he looked up from a gleaming mass of metal, annoyed at the interruption. Putting the finishing touches to his own invention of a micro-telescope, destined, he hoped, to outclass all known microscopes by something like 3,000 diameters, he had no desire to have his concentration disturbed. Irritably, he snatched the phone to him.

"What is it?" he snapped impatiently, and, to his surprise, Nick Easton's voice came over the wire.

"That you, Gordon? Say, listen, something terrible's happened! The whole institute has gone up like a powder magazine! Surely you heard it?"

Wood started and forced himself to think. He had heard a remote explosion, now he came to think of it. But, being fifteen miles from the institute and absorbed in his work, he had thought little more of it.

"I'll come at once," he answered quickly. "Meet me there."

He cast one last regretful look at his instrument; he would have to postpone his first test of its powers, after all. Ten minutes later his car had brought him to the scene of the disaster and, finding Nick, he stood with him and watched the immense blaze, sorrowfully watched thousands of dollars' worth of equipment going up in smoke. Nor was that all. Other buildings nearby, smashed irreparably by the disaster, were blazing fiercely.

"What the devil could have caused it, I wonder?" Nick muttered, his face troubled in the glare. "Any ideas, Gordon?'

"Plenty," the scientist answered cryptically. "There were no combustibles or anything of that nature in the building—no chemicals that could catch fire. There was only that damned piece of metal in the cellar. Somehow it brought this about; nothing else could cause so terrific an explosion. If that is so—"

He stopped and frowned heavily.

"Well?"

"There's plenty that might happen. That stuff was un-Earth-ly—it belonged to an age long past, when life first spawned in the universe. It has a life of its own, of a sort—or rather did have—maybe intelligent life beyond our scale of reasoning—either too high or too low—but, also, in common with all other forms of protoplasmic life, even though it was metallic instead of cellular, it could not be destroyed completely.

"For instance, if one were to blow protoplasm to pieces there would be some fragment that would escape and that would rapidly grow up again. Here we are dealing with electric-ity of unimaginable power, utterly beyond our comprehension. The damned stuff has blown up, that we know, and probably released something equivalent to subatomic energy in normal matter. That means it's still probably alive in some fresh form; it is obviously indestructible by very reason of its nature.[1] It lives on the basic element of the universe itself."

"You know about the overhead car wires, of course?"

"What about them?"

Nick turned in surprise. "Why, I thought you knew! They're out of action. I tried to get a car down here, but I had to walk it. Look around and see for yourself. One or two people tell me that the power failure, which seems to have spread to the elevated as well, almost coincided with the explosion."

"It did, eh?" Wood's face set; he swung around actively. "That gives us a lead, anyhow. We're heading for the power houses right now. Come along with me; I want first-hand infor-mation on what happened."

Nick followed him to the parked car. For fifteen minutes they moved slowly through milling throngs of people; then, at last, they were in the clear. Ten minutes of speeding brought them to the main power station. Wood, knowing the place from long experience, streaked up to an emergency exit and burst into the hot, noisy interior with Nick behind him. Without hesitation, he singled out Donovan, chief engineer.

"Oh, hello, Mr. Wood!" He was clearly surprised at the scientist's sudden appearance. "What's your trouble?"

"Never mind my trouble; what about yours? What's all this about the power stopping?"

"Rarest thing I've ever struck!" he declared flatly. "The darn machines are running as sweetly as they ever did, but there's no power going from them! That's what we can't figure out. Somewhere there's a fault. There's *got* to be one! We're trying right now to find it."

"You've no theories?"

"None. In forty years I never knew anything like this. Thank goodness, the lighting section wasn't affected! That seemed to escape."

Wood nodded slowly. "How long will your examination take?"

"About another hour maybe. Can't tell. Why?"

"I'll stick around until you're through. I want to see what happens."

"O.K." The engineer shrugged and turned back to his work of supervision.

Wood turned quietly to Nick. "If they can get going again perhaps we can see if that darned stuff is still in action," he muttered. "It's quite obvious now that it absorbed all this juice and then blew up. If it's still in existence in some other form, it—"

He stopped and looked up sharply. The lights in the lofty ceiling were flickering and wavering strangely, like candle flames caught in a draft. The engineers looked up, too, astounded. That the lights in the very power house itself should behave fractiously was a mortal sin, an unforgivable slight on their reputations.

"What in hell—" Donovan began, then his sentence evaporated into speechless dismay, as every bulb suddenly dimmed down to red-hot filament and then slowly expired. The great place sank gently into darkness. And yet, oddly enough, the mighty generators in the adjoining power-room section were roaring as powerfully as ever.

"Quickly!" Wood snapped, springing into life. "Get a torch, Donovan. I want to see those other generators."

"Right!" The engineer blundered around in the dark, then presently snatched a torch from some accustomed spot. Its penetrating pencil abruptly stabbed the gloom. Rapidly, he led the way into the adjoining wilderness of thundering machinery.

Tight-lipped, Wood stared at the output meters, cast his eyes over the whole array of white-faced dials. When he turned he could dimly behold Donovan's astounded face.

"By hell!" Donovan swore thickly. "Every darned meter down to zero! No load is going through! Say, Wood, what is all this about?" He clutched the scientist's arm almost appealingly. "This is against all reason. These machines are functioning as perfectly as the others, but no power is being generated. *Why?*"

"Shut them off," Wood ordered, curtly. "The juice is being absorbed. It will prevent further supplies if you stop generating. Hurry!"

Somewhat bewildered. Donovan obeyed, pulled out massive master switches, then stood waiting for the next. The generators droned to a standstill. In the torchlight Wood's face was set and determined.

"Listen," he said grimly. "You guys will be able to figure out what I'm going to tell you much quicker than ordinary people. There's something loose that feeds on electricity. We had it in the research institute before it blew up. There's the fear now that it may do something more than just consume juice. Being electrical energy of some kind, of a type never known on Earth before, it is likely that it will upset our own electrical systems completely. Did you ever hear of living electricity?"

"Like a live rail?" Donovan hazarded heavily.

"Lord, no! I mean alive—like us! Able, probably, to think?"

"Say, Mr. Wood, what are you getting at?" Donovan demanded bluntly. "Are you trying to tell us that you scientific guys over at the institute have made something out of electricity that thinks?"

"We had nothing to do with it, but a professor out in California had. He tried to make matter out of energy, and there is much to prove that he probably succeeded. That stuff in our cellars was the result of his experiment, and if, as we believe, it was primordial electric protoplasm, it represents life as it *should* be in the universe, instead of our own absurdly limited little forms. Flesh and blood isn't the only thing that can think, you know. And remember this! All of us are electricity when it comes to rock bottom.

"Chance made it that certain cosmic wave lengths produced life and intelligence in carbohydrates and phosphates, which caused us to evolve from mere slime to our present status. An infinitely shorter wave length, the one which brought our universe into being, could produce the same effect in metal, but once more electricity would be the basis, just as it is with us. So you see, I fear that this stuff, even though blown asunder, has released its strange energy in the form of radiation, and is, in consequence, reforming and re-patterning all things of an electrical nature on the Earth. The more electricity it gets, the stronger it becomes."

"But it isn't possible to make matter out of energy!" Donovan snorted.

"1 agree with you that it has never been done before—but this time we are quite confident that Professor Draycott *did* accomplish it! Hence the danger!"

The engineer scratched his bald head. "I reckon I can't make sense out of it, Mr. Wood. What's worrying me is how we get this darned electricity back into shape. You say there's something electrical upsetting us? Well, why don't we find it and—and exterminate it?"

"About as simple as rubbing out a shadow with an eraser," said Nick. "We can't get at it. It's radiation. Isn't it, Gordon?"

"Of a sort." He nodded worriedly. "Frankly, we don't know what the devil it is. Like electricity, we don't know its real nature, but we do know its effects. Later we may be able to form some idea about it. In the meantime, I shall do all in my power to sort the thing out—rest assured on that. Keep the generators off until you get further orders. This isn't just an ordinary break-down; it's a case where everybody will have to take their orders from the scientists. We'll have to establish fresh headquarters, to start with. Temporarily, we can use my home."

"I get it." Donovan nodded, though he was obviously still puzzled. He looked down at the torch in his hand. "Funny that a whole power house fails and yet this little thing keeps burning, isn't it?"

"No, it's quite natural," Wood answered quietly. "This un-known quantity, as we'll call it, is absorbing the vaster quanti-ties first. Things like that torch battery will go later. But now I've got to get going. There's plenty to do. Come on, Nick."

Donovan lighted the way back to the emergency exit; then the two scientists passed into the darkened metropolis. Every-where was incredibly gloomy; there was only the starshine for illumination. Where formerly the city had been ablaze with the lights of the late evening, there was now not a single glimmer.

III.

New York accepted the city-wide black-out with the calm philosophy of good citizens. There was no panic, but there was a good deal of pickpocketing as audiences left movie houses and theaters to the illumination of guttering candles.

In many ways it was considered a unique experience to come out into a city utterly dark. Those who still possessed gas lights in their homes and shops smiled in a superior way and commented sagely on these new-fangled electric gadgets that were always getting out of order. In other quarters radio-station engineers were frantic with dismay, and so were ardent listeners whose particular programs had suddenly stopped dead.

The major emotion of philosophy and good-humored banter changed later to a definite irritation, when it was found that there were no street cars, and no subway or elevated trains. People stampeded the various stations, lost themselves in cavernous darknesses, and in the subway in particular there would have been tragedy had not the police come on the scene with small, portable searchlights.

Little by little, it was forced upon everybody's knowledge that the electricity failure was a very real thing; but even then they were not permitted to know that the engineers behind it were as baffled as they were. They walked home with mixed feelings; others' feelings were far more than just mixed when they realized how many floors they had to go up without an elevator.

Beyond question, the most worried man in the city was Wood himself and, in a lesser degree, Nick Easton. Practically all through that amazing night they were kept busy answering telephone calls from other employees of the institute, and particularly from Dr. Simon, managing director of the concern. Like most managing directors, he wanted to know the why and wherefore and only just stopped being abusive when Wood reiterated wearily that he couldn't explain the matter.

"We'll have to think up some excuse," Nick said. "Old Simon and his fellow directors won't believe that the explosion just happened. As chief scientist, Gordon, you might be in a spot."

"Spot, hell!" the irritated scientist retorted. "That's trivial, anyhow. The whole works has gone up—yes. So what? That isn't what concerns us. It's this devilish electricity that confounds me. How do we even begin to get at it?"

"Since all electricity is cut off, doesn't it stand to reason that there will be no increase in the strange power of this unknown quantity?" Nick asked presently, his face thoughtful in the candlelight.

"No—that's the pity! A power such as has been unleashed can take so many diversified forms when we realize that everything is really electrical. Since it can convert the power of an entire power station to itself, assimilate it into its own radiative form, it stands to reason that, as it attains a fresh balance or state of progress in its evolution, it will include almost everything material, because everything material is electric." Wood paused and looked at his friend grimly.

"Nick, it means that we are facing destruction!" he said slowly. "Our life will be usurped by the form of life that should have dominated the universe had not chance brought us into being instead. Thinking energy!. Intelligent electricity! Good heavens! Who'd ever have thought of it?"

"And impossible to reach!" Nick muttered.

"We can only watch. We may think of something, but from the very nature of the thing we're fighting I very much doubt it!"

* * * *

Whilst Wood tried to see some solution to the problem, whilst the people of New York slept in darkened rooms, whilst the remains of the research institute died down to glowing embers, slow and incredible changes were taking place in the very structure of the city—changes in the basic forms of earth and atmosphere that had never happened since time began.

When Dr. Andrews had believed that the creation of matter out of energy might produce far-reaching and perhaps devastating effects, he had only touched the very fringe of imagination. He could never have foreseen that vast shuffling of atoms, that bending of electronic orbits, the slow expansion of molecules, and the movement of unknown radiations.

The electrical energy of the exploded matter had, at the explosion, released itself in the form of radiation, but of a type totally different from any known on Earth or in the universe since matter had begun. Draycott had provided the key to a locked door, given birth to a form of matter which Nature, in her wisdom, had chosen to leave in abeyance.

What had been the purpose in giving motivation and thought to lifeless carbohydrates in the beginning no man knew—but now that was at discount, was no longer a stable and accepted thing, but a random element in the midst of a new and inexplicable change. For, in its steady expansion, in its rapid evolution from lowly electric energy to a form of radiation defying comprehension, the unknown quantity had begun to reassemble all the electricity about it in just the same fashion as the first living men had taken to their caves to hide from the rigors of the Glacial Epoch.

It was a metamorphosis unseen, evident only at first in the failure of all electricity. Man could not be expected to see the reshuffling going on under his very nose; could not possibly note the gradually expanding area of the unknown element. He only became aware of an invisible interloper in his midst on the following morning, when the city awoke to the day's work. It was forced on his attention by little but frequently recurring instances, at first almost unnoticed, then demanding observation by reason of constant repetition.

Here and there buildings were different. The stonework had changed to a most peculiar yellow shade instead of the normal gray—or, in the case of the whiter, newer edifices, there was a distinct streak of green in their midst—a strange and oddly shimmering green that swirled and eddied with indefinable beauty, and yet which seemed to be deep within the stone instead of merely on the surface. Curious people touched the stone, to find it as hard as ever. It was, as one bright reporter put in his newspaper—printed by hand presses owing to the failure of electric supply—like "socking a mist on the jaw and finding the jaw, amazingly enough, to be very hard!"

In particular, it seemed, was the Ranbury Building affected, owned by the famous Silas Ranbury, financial magnate. Perhaps because it was the nearest large edifice to the institute disaster of the night before, it was one of the first to be really disturbed. Certainly remarkable things happened to it.

Ranbury himself arrived at eleven in the morning, muttering uncomplimentary things about broken-down elevators; then, from force of habit, jabbed the bell push on his desk. Since it was connected to the electric mains it failed to work. Dark with gathering rage, he strode ponderously into the adjoining office and yelled for his secretary.

Miss Chester, angular, and usually very collected, swung a pair of bovine eyes upon him and remained exactly where she was—at her desk. Her expression was easily the strangest Ranbury had ever seen on any woman's face.

"Perhaps" I can get some attention here," he said sourly, from the doorway. "What in hell is the matter with everybody?"

He strode in impatiently, then stopped in sheer amazement. His eyes popped as he surveyed the empty space where tables and desks and staff should have been. His eyes shuttled up and down, the emptiness.

"Miss Chester, who gave the staff permission to move out of here and take the furniture with them?" he asked. "Answer me, can't you?"

Still Miss Chester did not move. She seemed to be trying to speak, and at last she managed it, in a series of gasping jerks.

"Sir—there is something terrible going on in here! The—the others just melted into thin air! And the desks and chairs'!"

"What!" The financier's brows came down fiercely. "Now, listen to me, Miss Chester. I want an explanation of this removal of furniture. I've had quite enough for one day! Where the devil is everybody? Hurry up and tell me—there's work to be done! Come now or—"

"I can't, sir!" Miss Chester nearly screamed. "I don't know what's happened. I'm—I'm ill, I think."

"Ill, eh? Stuffy atmosphere in here, I suppose." Ranbury scowled and turned to the window. With a flourish he flung it open, then turned back to the now wailing woman. A violent start shook his ponderous body.

She was there, yes, but what in Heaven's name was happening to her?

She was—yes, *smeared!* That was it!

As though her clothes and body had all run together in the most astounding, nauseous fashion. Then the chair and desk began to behave in the same way—danced and shimmered like creations of wax before a blazing fire instead of being solid metal.

Even as Ranbury stood there, transfixed, the whole combination, woman included, congealed into a shapeless, gleaming mass. Then it gradually vaporized and left nothing but thin air. For a moment Ranbury was conscious of a tingling pain shooting through his body—and that was all. His last scrap of office furniture, and secretary, had gone!

"What—what in thunder—" he began blankly. Then this eyes turned to the walls. They were smearing now, mysteriously, inevitably. He could see little saffron streaks creeping through their grayness, spreading out like arteries: Again came that decided tingling sensation.

He staggered forward a few steps, intent on leaving the office—but he never succeeded in doing it. At lightning speed the wall suddenly smudged and melted exactly as the furniture and secretary had done—soundlessly, and with devastating efficiency. In consequence, not only the entire thirty-seven-story Ranbury Building disappeared into the air, but the whole block on which it stood as well! The well-known spot was left completely empty, and in its stead stood a vast crater penetrating deep into the bowels of the Earth.

Police and reporters swept to the scene at top speed; people gazed down into the abyss, doubting the evidence of their own senses. Reporters cursed the uselessness of telephones and raced back to their newspaper offices. Hardly had they done so than runners arrived with the news of the disappearance of other buildings in the near vicinity, and of all the people inside them. Always it seemed to be the more modern ones that suffered, perhaps because of the greater complement of metal. But that the change was also spreading to the older ones was no longer in doubt, if their shimmering play of colors was any guide.

* * * *

Gordon Wood, in the meantime, in close touch with events was playing host to the dubious directors of the late research institute. Literally, having no place to go, they had come to the scientist's residence, at his request, to review the situation.

"Gentlemen, it is worse than I thought," Wood said grimly. "The whole face of the city is being patterned afresh. Three buildings gone in one day, together with the loss of countless lives. Electricity still refuses to work. Business is paralyzed because of it."

"How do you reason out the disappearances, Wood?" Simon, the managing director, asked heavily. He was not a scientific man, hardly even imaginative. Blond, sixty-two, and round-faced; he was concerned with the finances of science, not its ideals.

"They're not very difficult to explain. The exploded matter changed into radiation, or energy, just the same as ordinary matter would have done. In this case an unknown form of energy was released. It is conforming the foundations of material life to suit itself, attacking first the metallic substances. When the assimilation is complete and the new electronic formations formed, matter as we know it ceases to be, and there is emptiness. But I don't believe it is really emptiness—only invisible radiation."

Wood paused, leaned impressively forward across the table.

"Little by little, unless we can find a way around the situation, this energy will assimilate everything to its own level, destroy what centuries of evolution have built up. It will change not only the ordered pattern of the Earth, but that of other worlds and, maybe, the whole universe. And why? Because it is a matter-energy state that has not been active before. Now it is evolving, and ultimately it may become possessed of thought. When that happens all material life will have vanished, and the true life that was intended for our universe will have come into being."

"And what, do you suggest as a possible remedy?" Simon demanded.

Wood shook his head slowly. "There isn't one!"

"Come, come, Wood, that's absurd! You don't suggest that we are to be dictated to by an unknown element? Science can conquer anything."

"It can conquer most things, I know, but not such a thing as this. No man knows how to begin. How is one to begin to attack an unseen radiation, an evolving form of energy that can change the very electrons of life into a new pattern of its own, that can wipe out the most material creation as though it never existed? No, gentlemen, the more the thing is studied the more complex it becomes. I will try and get into touch with other scientists in the unaffected parts of the world and see if they have any suggestions. The only way to do it, since radio and submarine cable are paralyzed from this end, is to send fast airplane messengers. That. I have already taken the liberty of doing, warning other countries as well. When I have their conclusions I might be able to do something. "Until then—"

"We sit and wait!" the managing director said. "A damned nice state of affairs!"

* * * *

That same evening a thunderstorm of tremendous intensity burst over New York. None of the flurried, baffled populace had much idea where it had come from; they were too harassed by the events of the day.

It was nevertheless, a storm of bewildering force that it made itself noticed by the most nerveless temperament. It started just before midnight and continued in crashing, blazing furies of elemental madness until nearly dawn. New York was ablaze with bolts of lightning, shaken to its foundations by the frightful detonations of thunder. Then, toward sunrise, it began to abate; a weak daylight filtered upon an incredibly changed city.

Many of the taller buildings had been blasted down by lightning; others had completely disappeared in the same mysterious fashion as the day before; but most amazing of all was the presence, in unexpected places, of towering masses of smooth-faced metal, gleaming, dull gray in the morning light.

To their summits, these masses stood eight hundred feet or more, their various facets cut so smoothly that they instantly revealed their strange nature. No man could possibly have had a hand in them—not even Nature, for as a rule Nature is haphazard and careless with her efforts; she never cuts out a creation with razor-like sheerness.

Wood, Easton, and the other scientists, together with the directors, were not the only people who stared upon those astounding creations that morning; but they were at the forefront of the multitude that swarmed from every quarter of the city to try to discover what it was all about.

Buildings, it was found, were still swirling with that strange re-patterning light. Some of them vanished even as they were watched. Here and there isolated human beings disappeared, too. But devastating though these occurrences were, they paled into insignificancy beside the new happening.

Returning home, having made arrangements for the populace to keep clear of the substance, Wood endeavored to explain it to his puzzled associates.

"We may assume, I think, that the re-patterning is taking definite form," he commented. "Obviously the buildings and people that have been vaporized, the electric energies that have been absorbed, have had to form into a fresh state. Last night that state must have been reached, and this strange form of energy rebuilt itself into material substance identical with that which Draycott originally made. In consequence, we have these faceted pieces of matter, so beautifully cut that they express, somehow, an intelligent motivation behind it all. The more I see of this confounded stuff the more I get that it really does think!"

The others said nothing; it was obvious that they doubted the fact.

"I can't see why the darned stuff suddenly decided to turn itself into matter," Nick remarked. "Why the devil didn't it do that at first, instead of existing as free energy?"

"You might as well ask why primeval protoplasm didn't turn into a thinking animal right away. It had to evolve to that state, and when, finally, it attained that stage the effect was complete and resolved. So it is here! All this time, whilst things have been disappearing, whilst electricities have been absorbed, this radiation has been progressing, and last night that thunderstorm obviously represented a change in its state when it achieved solidity. The result is those lumps of matter. The process is still going on. Larger and larger matter formations will occur, and ultimately we shall find ourselves overpowered by this new form of matter life. If I could get hold of some of it, I might be able to analyze it and devise a means of destroying it."

"All right, then, let's get some of the metal!" the managing director snapped. "What the devil are we wasting time for?"

Wood said nothing to that. He realized more clearly than anybody the extreme caution necessary in attacking the strange substance. Besides, the drills he proposed using might themselves be converted into energy; the only thing against the possibility was that the lumps of metal might be in a comparatively quiescent state for the time being. So he decided to take a chance and made arrangements for steam-driven drillers and clampers to get to work.

Then, toward late afternoon, the public cleared away by police, he, in company with the others, watched operations anxiously.

At the end of two hours, powerful though the drills were, they only succeeded in hacking off a piece three feet square. Immediately, there was a rush toward it.

"Wait!" Wood yelled hoarsely: "Stand back! Don't touch that metal if you value your lives! Heh, Casey!" He swung round to the clamper driver. "Use your clamps on this stuff and drop it into that insulated steam wagon. I'll take care of the rest."

"O.K.," Mr. Wood."

The order was obeyed and the precious piece of metal duly deposited in the waiting wagon. Wood and the others vaulted up beside the driver, and the heavy vehicle began to return to the center of the city, finally arriving at Wood's private laboratory at the back of his home. The wagon was backed round, the metal tipped out onto the concrete floor via the window. Once that was done, Wood felt safe to act, but he took good care to keep his distance from the fragment as he began to move an instrument into position.

"What's the idea?" asked the managing director curiously.

"A microscopic examination," Wood replied quietly, "This instrument here is my own invention—a telemicroscope—and so far it hasn't had a test. I've spent years making it; it works on the principle of trapping and sifting light rays from the object to be examined, but the magnification is roughly three thousand times greater than the best microscope in existence. Besides, its principle makes it possible to view an object at a distance, which is exactly what we need in this instance. Here goes!"

He jammed his eye to the powerful series of lenses and swung the instrument round until it was fully trained on the brightly sun-lighted piece of metal on the floor. Time and time again he made minute adjustments, fitting lens after lens, finding the piece of metal becoming larger and larger under the increased power.

Then, at last, his breath caught sharply. He pushed his eyes even closer to the shaded eyepiece and stared unbelieving.

"Good—heavens!" he jerked out at last, and looked up astounded. "Nick! Tell me if you see what I see!"

Easton jumped to look, then swallowed hard in his throat. Under the extreme power of the lenses the metal was no longer metal but a mass of interstitial substances, a metallic honeycomb surging with life completely invisible to the naked eye. Spots of light, tiny points of incandescent brilliance, were moving with incredible speed, never once colliding, but conveying the impression of colossal hurry. It was like a strange, dark sea of living beings, a tiny universe of swirling worlds.

"Planets—or people!" Nick exclaimed at last.

"What!" Dr. Simon expostulated, and leaped forward. "Let me look!"

The scientists stood aside and allowed him to do so. When he looked again, his round face was utterly amazed. "What *is* it?" he gasped blankly.

"Life!" said Wood very slowly, frowning. "Life! A life such as we never expected to see on Earth. The *first* life, the *real* life, life within matter! No longer just an inert state, no longer matter that is ductile and malleable in our hands, but living, electrical life—the very core of the universe itself."

"I don't understand. Make it clearer, man!"

"It's simple enough. You see, until all this happened every form of inert matter such as—at random—stones, iron or gold—were purely inactive substances with no motivated, intelligent life of their own. Composed entirely of atomic formations complete with electrons and protons, the number of electrons varying, of course, according to the element concerned. They were the products of a half-finished experiment by Nature.

Somewhere in the dim past wave lengths came together and coincided, and the outcome was inert matter. Before that wonderful happening could be pursued to its conclusion the state ceased and left a universe filled with blazing forms of matter and a vast amount of empty space.

"The pattern of infinity was incomplete. Later, we may assume, another chance combination of radiations came together and excited the inactive carbohydrates of certain cooling worlds, our Earth amongst them, into chemical activity. Protoplasm came and, cycles later, intelligent man. But through all this wonderful process the inanimate form remained inanimate—unintelligent—waiting for that one chance to happen which would enable it to find itself.

"Draycott, all unwittingly perhaps, brought that one chance into being again. He found the chance combination of radiations, and inanimate matter began to live again. First, two energies combined to form the first matter; that exploded into intraatomic energy and released itself; it then 'digested' everything electrical and patterned itself as surely as the primeval amoeba patterned our present world. Finally, evidently reaching a peak in its evolution, it changed its state into one compatible with its surroundings, and visible matter arrived on our world. But it is different from ordinary matter in that life teems inside it, active life that is perhaps intelligent, and which, because it has all the basic powers of infinity to work on, will easily overthrow us.

"We exist on a border line. A happy chance put us there. But here we have a life that nothing can affect; life as it should be, unaffected by heat or cold, air of vacuum, distance or pressure, or even death. Electrical energy can never die so far as we know. So, we gaze on the first life, pursuing beyond doubt the purpose Nature really intended before she slipped up on the job and produced us instead."

"Then—then the Earth will be changed?" Simon faltered.

"Every form of matter as we know it will be changed," Wood answered grimly. "It will all break down into an energy state and be reformed into living matter. Ultimately we shall have a universe as it was intended to be, and not a haphazard, incomputable emptiness dotted with pointless spots of matter."

"But, say, why is it progressive?" Nick asked in puzzlement. "Why is it that the initial expansion and formation is still going on?"

"Why not? Since all the universe is electrical in nature, the new life has an inexhaustible supply. It uses electricity in all its forms to further its own ends, be they cosmic rays, heat rays, X rays, sunlight, unknown waves in the ether— It utilizes them all and naturally changes them to supply a favorable balance to itself."

"And to destroy it?" the managing director asked tentatively. "Have you found a way now you've examined the stuff?"

Wood shrugged futilely. "No. It can't be destroyed. One might try to destroy ordinary life itself just as easily. It couldn't be done. We shall have to advise the people of the entire world exactly what has happened. We are forced to prepare for the end. Electricity is the only weapon we could use and that is, obviously, useless. Firstly, because we haven't any to use, and secondly, because, even if we had, this damned substance would eat it all up. No. It means a slow and inevitable changing of the whole nature of things, the rapid progression of the first life to its ultimate destiny!"

IV.

Be it said to Wood's credit that he did make every effort to warn the people of the world what was taking place; In New York, of course, center of the trouble, he was readily believed and thereby precipitated the most amazing happenings.

According to temperament, there sprang up riots, prayer meetings, Judgment Day seekers, tub thumpers, and soap-box orators. Crime swept the metropolis in a devastating wave. Knowing that life was doomed to extinction, certain of the population gave way to all their secret lusts and villainies; in consequence, murder and rape reared their ugly heads in the shadows.

In other parts of the world there was flurry, bustle and anxiety. America was a suddenly dead continent, untouchable by wireless or telephone, manifestly in the grip of a great unknown. Boards of trade huddled together and tried to imagine what had happened to international relationship. Money markets shattered; the whole structure of civilization began immediately to totter at the foundations. Frantic people pelted steamship offices with inquiries; the telephone company was inundated with a flood of demands as to what had happened to the Atlantic submarine cable. In every country big business men chewed on their cigars and worriedly watched their tottering fortunes. Never before had there been such incredible catastrophe.

In the meantime, totally unaffected by the fears and concerns of petty humans, lords of the border line of creation, the strange metamorphosis of elemental power went on. By degrees New York began to evaporate, and, also, by degrees, in exact proportion, new metallic matter formations appeared. The whole face of the city changed within a week of the initial explosion at the research institute.

From the approximate center of New York the disturbance spread with lightning rapidity to Long Island, Brooklyn and New Jersey. The old, familiar sky lines vanished completely, and instead became irregular hills of metal. Overnight, almost, Brooklyn was joined to Manhattan Island by a solid mass of metal, metal so highly energized, so teeming with electrical life, that to go within two miles of it meant certain transmutation into the new element.

Hence, disaster certain throughout America, there began a tremendous exodus to other countries. But, at best, it was only staving off the evil hour. Through the days and weeks the influence spread inevitably.

Wood and Nick Easton left America with the other fugitives and made straight for London. They found the usually complacent English in a state of intense panic. They realized now that disaster was indeed coming, and something of the horror that had engulfed America began to sweep over the British Isles. It was the utter hopelessness of the situation that caused such trouble. There was nowhere on Earth to which anybody could go and be safe. Ultimately, destruction would catch up.

And the farther the trouble spread the faster it seemed to act. Within the space of six weeks all America and Canada had succumbed, were covered with irregular plains of dully gleaming metal that extended way out into the Pacific on one side and the Atlantic on the other.

The change was coming very close indeed to English shores. The influence was already upon those green islands, instanced by the abrupt failure of all electric apparatus and the vanishing of buildings.

Overnight the unknown quantity stepped into the midst of the country, but, unlike its haphazard efforts in New York, when it had striven to attain a balance, it moved now in an advancing tide, evaporating everything in almost a straight line, reforming into matter after a short interval, then going on again.

Throughout the terrible night when the unknown quantity really entered England, panic-stricken people moved in yelling multitudes through every quarter of the country. Some flew to the isolation of the open; others raced for the company of other people, but all of them were inevitably trapped.

Wood was with Nick when the disaster reached him. With the calm philosophy of true scientists, they knew only too clearly the futility of trying to escape from the enemy. So they waited for it to come to them, seated on a form on the Thames embankment, overlooking the major bulk of the city in the calm light of early dawn.

It was hard to believe that there was anything wrong when they looked northward. Southward, however, there was no London—only a vast and hazy expanse of metallic desert that crawled visibly forward. The city's prosperity had ended. No vehicles were moving. Only the sound of shouting, terrified people was in the air.

"Well, I guess it's finally caught up with us, Nick," Wood commented with a twisted smile. "The human life has had a good run; now it's the turn of the proper life. It won't be long now!"

Nick nodded slowly; it was unaccountably hard to face death complacently. Wood was the elder man, far more incisive and philosophical than his partner.

"It doesn't seem right—" Nick began almost hotly, then paused as a pricking sensation passed through his body. It was as though countless thousands of needles were driving into him. He winced with pain, jumped up, staggered forward a step. He caught a glimpse of Wood's strained, set face, gleaming with sudden perspiration. He said no words—simply pitched forward from the form very abruptly and lay still on the flagstones.

"Gordon!" Nick shouted desperately. "Gordon, old man—"

He lurched dizzily. Confound this pain! He moved forward a step to pick his friend up, but by the time he had forced himself that far, Gordon Wood was no longer there; he had evaporated utterly into nothing, changed arid resolved into the unknown tide.

Nick shouted again, huskily. Behind him a metallic incredibility was fast forming. The violent, pricking pains increased. A conviction of inexorable pressure drove into every nerve, until, head reeling in swimming blackness, he, too, went crashing to the stones.

Within ten seconds his body had vaporized.

* * * *

With inexorable progression, the strange metamorphosis went on. It wiped out England utterly in the space of nine hours, and still went on implacably, resolving every human being, every scrap of landscape, every drop of water, every molecule of air, into one continuous condition of unbroken matter. Until at length the Earth resembled a rough-hewn ball of unjointed matter teeming with incredible new life.

From that point the insatiable substance still went on, following out the plan it should have followed in the beginning. It reached vast metallic arms into the deeps of space. Under the increasing weight the Earth collapsed completely and changed from a ball into a vast sea of matter floating in space, reaching out branching arms like some primeval amoeba, digesting and assimilating the constant flood of radiations sweeping the unplumbed depths of the void.

At length it covered the 93,000,000-mile stretch to the Sun, and wiped out that luminary completely, expanding enormously by the increase of electric energy to its strange formation. By inevitable degrees the now-frozen worlds of Mercury, Venus and Mars were obliterated.

The inner circle of the solar system was no longer empty space, but an incredible mass of matter in which space had been utterly swallowed up.

And, as it had been on Earth, its progress increased in proportion to its steady enlargement. It ate up the abysses and filled them with solidity. It engulfed the outer planets and extended its ramifications to the nearest stars. Onward and onward, forever breaking down and converting itself, through years—centuries—uncountable millenia.

The spatial universe began to disappear. Electromagnetic ether, so long the vague unknown to scientists, was instead patterned with new life. From the center to the extreme limits of the universe there came to be no space, only one vast dull-gray immensity in which life spawned in its most natural and yet most incredible form.

When—and only when—this stage had been reached, was the metamorphosis complete. Every scrap of available energy had been utilized and changed to suit the new energy's requirements. The required level had been gained and, just as man had found life when the equilibrium of the former universe had been reached, so the new form of life, that had existed as dimly intelligent electric power in the beginning, began now to take shape, to pattern itself into recognizable formation.

V.

The mind that had belonged to Gordon Wood of Earth, which had been suspended in faculty for an unknown time, began to stir slowly in a deep, unknown sea of impulses and suggestions. Out of the blackness there came the dawning light of new knowledge, and with it an intense remembrance of incredible events, of energy transforming into unknown matter.

As he arose out of this gulf he became aware of two things: one, that his body was a form of glowing, bluish energy; and, secondly, that he existed in an apparent endless sea of misty light, incredibly beautiful light possessing the misty translucence of a pearl. It came to him as a momentary shock when he realized that everything he saw was not accomplished by eyes, but by the pulsing of various forms of electric radiation. He had no nerves, no sexual power, no emotions, was nothing but a somewhat heavier form of the endless sea of pearly light surrounding him.

Spread in the distance before him, as he became more and more aware of his environment, vanishing into inconceivable distance, were other beings, gently moving spots of light pursuing, no doubt, their own purposes.

His mind went back to that unknown time when he had examined the fragment of metal in his laboratory. It had been populated by beings such as this, and now he was a part of them!

He was puzzled, faintly bewildered, but not afraid. He knew he had died and risen again, that his Earthly body had long since been resolved into a new type of energy, that his mentality had lived on, and, at last, taken on its individual power again after unknown intervals of suspension. He began to wonder whence came the electrical stimulus that fed him so constantly. That was beyond his understanding.

He thought of Nick Easton, wondered what had happened to him. Hardly had the thought formed in his mentality before he found himself abruptly propelled through the iridescence to come to rest not two feet from another glowing form identical to himself.

He tried to speak, remembered that he had no vocal cords, and instead thought of the words he intended to convey.

"Can you—can you be Nick Easton? That was?"

Immediately the answer came back, perfectly legible, the pure, sharp-cut essence of thought itself.

"I was Easton, yes. You're Gordon, of course? What do you imagine has happened to us this time? Look at all this— these countless millions of light spots. Undoubtedly they are intelligent. Do they possibly represent the vanished people of Earth?"

"I think I just begin to understand," Wood replied. "That matter life we saw forming, when apparent death overtook us, must finally have attained its level, and the new life came properly into being. Those electric creatures we saw in existence so long ago in that chunk of metal really represented just haphazard beings, without much intellect. Remember how they raced about so desperately, as though trying to figure things out? It was pure confusion! This is ordered, perfect symmetry.

"When an element reaches a perfect, equipoised state every one of its attributes and formations is in perfect tune with each other. The outcome is a flawless unity. Our old universe was never that way. It was a third inanimate matter, a third half-intelligent carbohydrate, and a third space. That explains, too, how it is that the instant I thought of you I found you. Perfect organization impelled me, literally, with the speed of thought, right to your side."

"And our exchange of communications without words?"

"What else but pure thought transference? Thought is electrical; therefore, it is the easiest medium of exchange. Remember how we tried it in the old days, and how we were hampered? There is much now that is being made clear."

"There must be others," Nick commented. "Suppose we try and find them?"

"Agreed," Gordon assented, and together they swept the endless abyss of pearly light. It was as they pursued their astounding journey that they began to more fully apprehend what had occurred.

There were not only Earthly minds in this vast expanse of electrical knowledge, but those of other worlds, of Mars and Venus and the giant outer planets, which formerly had existed in the various formations common to those worlds, but were now reduced to a common level. Then there were also the beings of the planets beyond the former ken of Earthlings, far away in the infinite depths of space.

It came to Wood, as he pursued his journey and exchanged communications with these varied denizens of long-forgotten worlds, how utterly different the new state of affairs was. Gone was the old muddling order; gone were the old struggles, the racial differences, the different levels of intellect, the uphill battles to try and understand.

Space was no longer a barrier; space and matter were now interwoven in the pattern nature had intended until chance had changed it. The universe was a spatial one no longer; only a form of matter which, to the electrical beings populating it, had all the appearance of pearly vapor. To them had been granted the power of passing through the very interstices of matter itself. Heat and cold, death and illness, were no longer their lot to bear; instead, they could exchange information with the more advanced ones, and gradually bring this new and amazing life into one of perfect concord.

Since there was no cognizance of time, now that visible matter was not in existence to them, neither Wood nor Nick Easton had the slightest idea how long it took them to gather together the major minds of this strange infinity. Perhaps it took them aeons; they did not know. But ultimately they had established a common union of thought wherein they began to realize the vast purpose that, before, had been left unfinished.

The accepted leader of the new universe, leader because of his clarity of thought, finally made clear the new existence in a thought transference to his multimillions of contemporaries.

"When the universe existed in its old state there was, of necessity a completely disorganized state of affairs that none of us could rightly understand. We did know, however, that electrons were the basic formation of matter. Therefore we knew that electricity was also the basic formation. What we could not correlate was the infinitely big with the infinitely small. There seemed to be no reason for vast emptiness in which matter flamed away to eternal death—and indeed there was none. It was an unfinished masterpiece. Various haphazard things took on the intelligence which we now have as a massed whole. We each lived and thought in our own particular little sphere, and tried to imagine what lay in the empty spaces beyond our particular galaxy.

"Now we know the truth. Thanks to a scientist of Earth, the mistake of the beginning has been rectified and the law of chance again operated. The universe now is filled from end to end with matter, and we are part of that matter, beings of electricity—we call it such for want of a better name—who, instead of reacting on the thoughts formerly given to us by the electrons comprising our beings, now operate purely as thought.

"Such things as electrons do not exist here; we know them now for what they were: purely the smallest expressions of thought, fragments left over from that great, unfinished attempt. We have proven that mind lives on eternally; but we could never understand why death broke the continuity. Now we know that it never did; that we would have continued to live in a series of fragmentary states, had not a chance happening resolved for us the real nature of the universe.

"We move now by the pure impulse of thought. There is no such thing as planets, no visible matter at all, no profound riddles, no barrier to distance. We are self-contained and need never puzzle again because, about us, ready to be summoned on the instant by pure thought alone, are the greatest minds of our former universe. The mysteries of creation, of energy, of matter, of inexplicable space time are all explained; we know now that they were merely erroneous concepts brought into being by our formerly unsuitable bodies and brains. That is why planets never could communicate with each other, why we found space a bar to our material progress, and that is why electricity was always, and is now, the basic power of thought and eternity."

"And the mind that gives us our minds?" asked Wood. "What of that?"

"Who are we to question the power that organizes infinity from end to end, who patterns eternity and draws the end of space together? We only know that we are a part of that purpose and mind, whatever it may be, and in the future we shall devote our interests in that direction, supreme in the knowledge that we have intellect and ordered unity that will make it possible. In the old state we could never have done it, never have glimpsed such a thing as this, but now that the metamorphosis is complete, and every intellect understands the other, there is nothing to block our path. Tirelessly, ceaselessly we shall strive toward that end."

With that, the master mind ceased its exposition. The matter universe flowed and vibrated with acquiescing thoughts; the entities broke up and divided into groups, to devise their own particular ways and means of pursuing their intellectual course to the limit.

As hitherto, Wood clung closely to Nick, exchanged views with him, weighed suggestions, devised plans all of which, along with those of the others, were tendered to the master mind for consideration.

Through Earthly multi-epochs, this perpetual arranging and planning went on, leading ever upward to a vital point, until, at last, every conceivable mind in that astounding universe was ready for the forward intellectual drive to the next higher stage—a state to be reached by the pure force of thought against that of existent matter, which, for all its negotiability, was still a mundane and not a pure-thought factor. The state of absolute intelligence had yet to be attained.

An intense calm settled on the assembled multitudes as they waited the given signal to concentrate on the one pre-devised union of thought. Wood waited in silence, Nick floating in disembodied blueness at his side.

Then came the master's signal, penetrating to the farthermost reaches of that colossal expanse of intelligence. Instantly, every thought was trained in one direction, concentrated on one particular point which, if resolved by the power of the thought, would mean the passing of even electricity and the attainment of the purely intellectual realm.

It seemed to Wood that a roaring broke on his impulsive senses, the first really Earthly noise he had heard since the new existence. It grew with the passing seconds; the electric beings of the universe gyrated and twisted in the most incredible fashion. Their bodies were decomposing, vanishing into the midst of the all-pervading pearly light. Like an expanding ball the disappearing area spread, having as its center the larger electrical personage of the master.

Faster and faster, a swirling enigma, expanding in a throbbing tide throughout the whole enormous area, until at last Wood found himself caught up in the midst of it. His mentality remained clear, but his electric body passed away in a haze of disintegrating blue light. Upon every hand blue explosions were hurtling away from him; the entire matter universe was quaking from end to end, falling in upon itself, collapsing completely.

Then there came a great and vivid light that burst suddenly through the midst of the ruptured matter universe, a searing tide of brilliance. Though he had no eyes, no body, only pure mental conception, Wood could distinctly see what was about him.

A machine! So colossal that it staggered even his abnormal perceptions. In appearance it resembled an Earthly generator, but its lowest point was infinitely higher than the old-time Mount Everest, and the rest of it towered into hazy remoteness and lost itself. Even as he looked, Wood could feel himself moving away from it as if on the crest of an etheric wave. He passed through the very interstices of another colossal machine, and still went on moving.

An incomprehensibly vast city was the next thing that smote his reasoning. His mentality reeled before it. A city populated by beings not entirely dissimilar to Earthlings, but of such stupendous size that he realized that, had he possessed his Earthly body, he would have been infinitely smaller than the smallest pin point by comparison.

He tried to fathom what these tremendous matter beings were doing, rushing about their city. Then, even as he tried to conjecture, he found himself suddenly and amazingly back again in a matter universe, filled once more with glowing electrical beings, but now considerably larger than before. He felt, too, a sudden and immense stimulus.

Vainly, he tried to imagine what had happened—how the procession of infinite concentration had brought about such an inexplicable state of affairs. Then the vibrations of the master came across the cross currents of astounded mentalities.

"That our universe was an atom in the matter formation of an infinitely vaster universe, we have long known," came his communication. "By the same rule, the primal atoms which Draycott created out of energy were also universes within ours. To make matter out of energy it was necessary for him to literally create universes on a small scale. That he did, and produced matter of an unusual form. That matter was unstable; the atoms or universes comprising it had to adjust themselves to the new conditions. They came, literally, out of anywhere into being.

"In accomplishing the adjustment, they upset every other universe or atom within *our* universe, and ultimately resolved the entire universe into a form of matter. We know how, in the beginning, we found the metallic element to be comprised of infinite living beings; that has been told to us. They were the beings of the atomic universes already annihilated! Now it has come to the stage where the effect has spread through our universe, which is—or was—really one atomic formation in the suprauniverse encompassing it.

"We have burst our own tiny atom much the same as that metal once burst itself in the research institute. How are we to know but what it burst by a process similar to ours, by concentration of thought from inside it, stimulated by the Earthly electricity around it? Our stimuli, clearly, has come from this suprauniverse's electrical machines. Our former universe existed inside a piece of metal, close to one of the immense machines of this suprauniverse. Could we examine it, we no doubt would find that its electrical powers have ceased.

"Whatever it may be, we know that our bursting our universe has destroyed an atom in this new universe, and that the energy thereof is re-patterning itself just as it did on Earth. We have formed again into matter, just as, back on the Earth, the mounds of matter formed when the right balance was struck. So it will go on through this world—the gradual annihilation of matter things and the replacement by those electrical—and from that upward and upward, through suprauniverses as yet undreamed of, a perpetual cycle of change—change—change!

"Ultimately it may bring us, after untold time, to our long-sought goal—pure thought. We know only one thing as yet: change the slightest particle of energy in any universe or world, and it will pass on through all universes, until the whole lot is resolved into an equal balance, so immovably linked is one universe with another. And to accomplish that process will take all eternity and—

"Yes, eternity!"

DARK ETERNITY

At the age of sixteen, Gregory Dunn was admitted as honorary member to the World Association of Psychology; at twenty-one he was professor extraordinary of advanced mental phenomenon in the New York Psycho-Institute; at thirty he was *the* acknowledged authority on the mind and its relation to the universe and humanity.

The people of 2040 listened to his lectures and read his many articles, realizing that in their generation had arisen a genius easily comparable to such past men as Archimedes, Copernicus and Einstein.

Dunn married at thirty-one. When his only son was twelve, he was teaching him the principles of his far-reaching discoveries, nurturing him on primers of psychology and its effects. In fact, it became increasingly obvious that Professor Dunn was a man with an obsession.

Aside from his normal professional life, he drove himself ceaselessly with furious energy upon ramifications of his art. To be a master of psychology was not sufficient for his restless, probing mind. He had to find the cause and effect of the very science he studied. To that end he devoted every waking moment—flogging himself at such a pace that friends and critics alike began to wonder how much longer his short, wiry body would stand the strain.

He labored in this fashion all his life, never taking a holiday, browsing among technical books, rereading and tabulating everything that had ever been written concerning the mind, working out numberless theories, some of them staggering enough in their import to astonish a nation, but by no means satisfactory enough for him.

Only once did he ease up through sudden grief at the death of his wife. Then he was back again, more ruthlessly determined than ever, hair a little grayer, powerful shoulders a little more stooped, an obsessed genius eternally striving, struggling, battling—for an elusive something.

He reached fifty-eight before young Allan graduated with honors at the Psycho-Institute and was able to become his assistant. Fresh and youthful, blond-headed, but unhappily with little of his father's rare genius, he endeavored to bind together many of the threads the older man had left scattered, knitting together theory with theory. But he only achieved the framework of the colossal idea his father was striving for.

Young Allan simply could not grasp the profound nature of his father's research. For hours he puzzled over it, blue eyes perplexed, strong young face drawn into a mask of concentration.

The Professor pored over sheet after sheet of figures, only looking up now and again to snap curt orders to the rest of the private laboratory staff in his employ. He rarely spoke to his son, not through any lack of sociability, but because his mind was so utterly preoccupied. He did, however, rise far enough out of his meditations one morning to snap almost rudely, "We don't get very far, Allan, while you stand around thinking! There's work to be done—lots of it. What's the matter with you? You don't see me lazing my time away!"

Allan came to earth with a start, then smiled a little. Going across to the desk, he flung an affectionate arm around his father's stooped shoulders.

"Not lazing, dad, and you know it! Just trying to figure out what you're driving at. Incidentally, don't you think you ought to take it easy for a bit? You're not a machine, you know, able to go—"

"Be damned, to that!" Dunn retorted, tight-lipped. "I've got a problem to work out before I depart this life, and I mean to do it! When I do finally move on, I want you to follow in my steps. That clear?"

"Of course," Allan said obediently. But his face was concerned as he noted the burning fervor in his father's sunken eyes, the unkempt white hair, the quivering hands clenched tightly on the sheets of figures. Energy—dynamic beyond belief—was still draining on that aging body and resolute brain.

"If only one could have eternity!" the older man whispered presently. "If only one could have the time to work out a problem instead of being overtaken by such a nuisance as death!" He stopped abruptly, then again became the curt, irritated scientist. "How far do you understand my theory, Allan?" he asked shortly.

"Not very far, I'm afraid. You've delved into the nature of mind more deeply than any man before you. I still cannot see what you are driving at. Maybe I'm dense, but—"

"Decidedly dense!" his father agreed, with an impatient snort. "I've weaned you on mathematics and psychology and you don't grasp the point of my researches! Yeu've knitted my theories together where I've slipped up, and still missed the point. Missed it!" he repeated explosively. "Damn it, boy, you must have grasped *something!*"

Allan hesitated briefly. "Well, I did grasp something, but it's so absurd I hardly dared to mention it. That monograph you put together about the co-relation of thought and matter— Did you mean to imply that they're both the same thing?"

"Of course I did! Different expressions of a monostate—that is to say that they are two distinctly evolved presentations of space. You cannot have mind without matter or matter without mind. The same fault that produced matter produced mind and the two are equally capable of annihilation to the point of them giving up their inter-energy."

"Both?" Allan shook his head. "That's the part that gets me, dad. You just can't annihilate mind! Science is perfectly sure of that!"

Dunn laughed cynically. "Science! You dare to stand there and say that to me? What has science ever contributed to my knowledge? Exactly nothing! It is what *I* have contributed to science that counts! I say that thought *can* be annihilated. I have no intention of actually doing such a thing, of course, but I do intend to release the subatomic energy of thought sometime before I die. To that end I have dedicated my life."

Allan stared into the half-mocking, glowing eyes. The old man grinned sardonically. "Can't take it in, eh?" He chuckled.

"I'll say I can't! No wonder I couldn't find out what you were getting at! But hang it, the subatomic energy of thought sounds—"

"That's what I said. I shall actually accomplish the feat before I'm through. Think of it! The energy of thought! Today it is a common affair to release the energy of an atom of matter; we span the globe with giant machines by the mere release of energy from several pounds of common sand. Since we have definitely proven the existence of power in matter, and since matter and mind are also interlinked, think of the release of thought energy from a single atom of thought!"

"But you can't!" Allan protested incredulously. "It's—it's fantastic! Absurd! You can't get hold of a thought and dissect it!"

"Now you're revealing your youth," the old man reproved. "For half a century I've devoted my time and energy to proving that I *can,* and no young cock sparrow like you is going to hint otherwise."

"But *how?* Thought is as intangible as—as a vacuum."

"To the normal sight and reason, yes," Dunn admitted. "But if you look around this laboratory, you'll see instruments which do far more probing than is possible to faulty human mechanism. Just as a thermopile can register the slight heat of the moon's surface, utterly undetectable to humans, so my specially fashioned instruments have been able to register the definite formation and vibration of the mind itself. It's anything but intangible, I assure you." He leaned back for a moment with a brief contented sigh. "Will old Maxwell's eyes pop when he sees what I've got!" he murmured.

So that was it! He was living for the opportunity to cut the ground from under the feet of his bitterest critic, Dr. Randolph Maxwell, master psychologist. After thinking for a moment, Allan said, "Suppose, just suppose, that anything were to suddenly happen to you? I know it sounds morbid, but we've got to face facts. What will I have to do?"

"If anything goes wrong with me before my research is complete, you'll do exactly nothing. I couldn't possibly cram fifty years of knowledge into your brain in a few weeks. Obviously you have not got my flair; genius usually does skip a generation."

"Maybe you're right there. But you'll surely tell me how you're going to accomplish this thought-energy release?"

Dunn shook his gray head. "No, Allan. For one thing, I have not the time now and, for another, I'm keeping quiet until I have every detail fixed. I don't think it will take very long the way I'm going on. You keep on working as you are and try to understand. Maybe you'll learn something of my methods. Then one day—one day I'll prove my point!" He meditated briefly, then resumed his notes. "Now get back to work!" he snapped out. "I want you to start assembling that machinery for me. Hurry, boy, hurry!"

* * * *

Gregory Dunn was proven to be too optimistic in his beliefs. His assumption that perfection of his scheme would come before very long vanished in thin air as weeks sped swiftly into busy months; as summer and winter came and went unnoticed; as months elongated into a year, then two years—and finally three.

But in that time Allan, stimulated by the few truths he had heard on that other distant morning, had given himself heart and soul to the task on hand, bringing every facet of his scientifically trained mind to bear upon it. The more he explored his father's research, the more he marveled.

The old man had actually eliminated all the vagaries connected with mental phenomenon and gone right to the central core of cause and effect. There was, of course, much that was puzzling, that would demand the old man's own elucidation. But in the main Allan began to discover that thought was no longer an abstract, unknowable state—a mystic font of all creation—but just matter in a different form at a different vibration.

Here and there, as he worked through the various postulations, he found concrete evidence of basic laws, supported by statements from such past experts as Eddington and Jeans—and further back still—Kant and Aristotle. Mathematics, thought, energy, time and space were more than interrelated. They were the varied products of the same thing, in much the same way as different species of animals and humans are, in truth, evolved offshoots of an original primal atom of matter.

So much Allan grasped of the theoretical side. The rest was still a mystery. He would have to wait the old man's full discourse to the masters of the profession—the discourse that Dunn hoped would wipe out all the opposing theories of the didactic Dr. Maxwell completely.

Allan found the mechanical side even more complicated. He worked entirely to his father's plans and in a newly equipped annex to the private laboratory, he began the erection of two immense cylindrical pillars, eight feet in width, insulated by succeeding layers of the most nonconductive materials known to science. At the top of each column was mounted a hollow globe—sixty feet in diameter—composed of highly polished aluminum.

Between the spheres themselves—held horizontally in a metal cradle hanging by chains from the lofty ceiling—reposed a vast vacuum tube, the central unit of one of the most efficient atom-disrupting machines ever made.

Both spheres, Allan judged, were to be the source of the atom smashing. Within them was heavy machinery—controlled from the laboratory generators and switchboards below—for carrying an endless series of minute electrical charges at 30,000-volt pressure, building up gradually within the spheres to a potential state and capable of achieving a maximum power of 17,000,000 volts each—nearly 4,000,000 volts higher than science had so far reached in its atom-smashing activities. Allan brooded upon the reason for such terrific power and once again could only assume that dealing with mental causes had something to do with it.

Clearly, the throwing of the master switches would release a combined force of 14,000,000 volts, maximum, from positive and negative terminals, sufficient to shatter completely any known matter placed inside the bombardment chamber of the vacuum tube.

In the tube itself—entry being gained from either of the two spheres—was a curiously fashioned globe of almost transparent metal, made in two flawless hemispheres and cramped immovably together by the four-sided grip of a powerful-jawed matrix. Welded through the cylinder were four terminals—designed to receive wire connections—converging on its inner side into brightly polished concave bowls, four in all, so designed that their combined foci pointed to the exact center of the ball.

Looking along the line of sight, Allan could distinctly observe that the bombardment of released energy would probably shatter the transparent sphere and hurl its results into the complicated receiving chamber beyond. But what was to be within the sphere? That was the point at which he balked—

Puzzled though he was, he went on steadily with the work, studying every part of the machinery as he went, supervising the assembly of the power generators and, in particular, a massive, straddling conglomeration of machines that, in basis, reminded him of those in force at a radio transmission station. In every instance, however, the myriad wire connections led to step-up transformers designed in series, connecting in turn with the major wires leading to the vacuum tube spheres.

Converging to a central transmission point, all the machinery seemed to have its main focus above a light aluminum chair—an absurdly orthodox thing in such a wilderness of engines—supplied with broad arms studded with numbered buttons and switches. Poised over the top of it was an odd, flawlessly balanced rotor composed of six fan blades, highly magnetized and made up of the same semi-transparent metal as the ball in the vacuum tube. When the thing was in action it would whir soundlessly over the head of anybody sitting in the chair, apparently transmitting its results—whatever they might be—to a minute microphonic pick-up in the box on top of it, and thence to the transformers.

Allan was convinced by the time he came to the end of the various erections that he knew less than when he had started. His father's privately acquired fortune must have been drained to rock bottom by the purchase of such devices. He found the old man still uncommunicative and only received grunts when he announced that the machinery was finished.

He was not even permitted to enter the great laboratory once his erecting task was over. But on many evenings afterward, he heard the thunderous, crackling roar of enormous energy discharges and could feel the brittle sense of static in the air as his father put the finishing touches to a lifetime of study and concentrated effort.

For he had at last gained the goal he sought. He became almost fanatically eager as he announced the fact exactly six weeks after the final completion of the machinery.

"I've got it, boy!" he declared, pacing nervously up and down the laboratory. "This is the thing man has been waiting for! A lifetime of work, but worth every hour, every second that I've packed into it. Tomorrow I demonstrate!" He looked up with quick decision.

"Of course you've invited Dr. Maxwell?" Allan asked rather dryly.

"All of 'em," Dunn said. "Maxwell, Van Linman, Crawford—they're the main ones. The others will come along as a matter of course. Tomorrow, Allan, I announce everything to the world—the cumulative result of my studies. It'll be your legacy, too, to use well and keep away from the hands of dabblers who don't know what they're doing."

"I'm afraid I know no more than they do in my present state of ignorance," Allan stated briefly. At that the older man looked vaguely shamefaced.

"Perhaps I have been rather selfish," he confessed. "Still, I have been so locked up in my work I've been disinclined to explained anything without concrete evidence. You know how it is! But now I have that evidence—the ultimate truth about mind!" He stopped, eyes gleaming speculatively; then he said briefly, "Take today off if you want, Allan. The demonstration takes place here at ten tomorrow. I have to fix some special materials in the vacuum globe, ready for tomorrow—brain material!" he said. Then he shuffled pensively away and left Allan staring wonderingly after him.

II.

Exactly at ten o'clock the following morning the scientists and newspapermen began to enter the demonstration laboratory. Professor Dunn greeted them one after another with a handshake and a faintly cynical smile on his face—a smile which broadened significantly as he shook the hand of Dr. Randolph Maxwell.

The tall, torpedo-bearded scientist looked at him keenly with his piercing gray eyes. "Trying to spring something new again, er, Dunn?" he asked. "I've made a long trip from Los Angeles, so it had better be good."

"It will be," Dunn assured him calmly. "If you will be so good as to take your reserved seat in the front row you will, I think, find your trouble in coming here amply compensated for."

With a rather indifferent shrug Maxwell moved slowly across to the railed section of seats, settled himself between Van Linman, the bald-headed psychologist, and Crawford, the atom annihilation expert. Both men kept their own counsel and disregarded the well-chiseled, decidedly cynical features of the expert between them. As a psychist Maxwell was superb; as a man he was a complete anathema, bitter to the point of hostility when confronted with theories that did not agree with his own.

At length the full assembly was complete. The gentlemen of the press sat in a section to themselves, silent but interested, speculative eyes on the grouped masses of machinery. Then their notebooks flashed into position for action as Dunn quietly closed the laboratory door and stepped forward, leaving Allan to supervise the waiting engineers.

"Gentlemen," the professor said quietly, clearing his throat, "I shall go directly into the nature of my theory, under the assumption that you know already, through the newspapers, about my machinery and its infinitely superior atom-smashing power. In the first place, as you well know, I have devoted my life to the study of thought. I have definitely proven that mind, matter, energy, radiation—anything you care to mention—are *all* evolved products of the same thing. They all sprang from the accident, the original fusion of radiant energy wave lengths of 1.3×10^{-13} cms, in the very core of commencing time and space."

"The conception is not altogether novel," remarked Maxwell, peering from under insolently drooping eyelids.

"I did not infer that it was!" Dunn retorted acidly. "But I do assert that thought is just as capable of being disintegrated as matter is. Like matter, it can be patterned into any desired form. Mind can become matter, and matter can become mind."

"Rank nonsense!" exclaimed Maxwell sourly; but he was alone in his condemnation. The others were listening intently, particularly Allan.

"In the first place," Dunn went on, ignoring the interruption, "matter is impossible without mind. Conversely, without mind there cannot be matter. That everything we know and understand is simply through external impression—transmitted through light waves and interpreted by the brain—is an old and accepted theory. Remove the process of sensation, sight, hearing, and all the physical attributes, and what have we? Nothing!"

"But we can still imagine plenty!" Van Linman put in quickly.

"You can only imagine something based on former experience," Dunn pointed out. "That you cannot disprove—not even you, Dr. Maxwell!"

The psychist smiled bitterly. "So far you've merely recited established facts, Dunn. You'll have to be more convincing than that."

"I will be. You will admit, no doubt, that the waves of probability of an electron shade off into other-dimensional space?"

Maxwell nodded, but his bearded lips said "Old stuff!"

"Very well. The correlation of that shading off occurs in mentality where it slides off into the subconscious realm. That state is identical with the electron's own veerage."

"An unique analogy, but hardly satisfying," commented Crawford. "You still evade the issue. The nature of thought, the—"

"I'm coming to it," Dunn interrupted. "Of necessity I have to go a long way round with such a subject. We know that our entire universe is naught but waves, be they light waves or electron waves. We know that the very basis of matter is purely waves. Certain of these waves reach visibility to our eyes and we call them matter. Be it a cabbage or king, it is still matter. But others of these waves, invisible to the human eye, but just as surely interconnected with matter, are the waves of thought, apprehended by only one organ in the body—the brain. And with those waves we can do things, things which include creation, hypnotism, mental telepathy, and so forth. We can give birth, mentally, to characters we have never known—take the great literary artist for example. And could we but understand these waves aright, we could instantaneously transform a mental creation into a matter creation, as surely as today we transform matter into pure energy."

"And, of course, you can do this?"

Dunn nodded slowly and stood smiling slightly at the chorus of gasps around him.

"It's absurd!" Maxwell cried hotly, rising up. "You dare to suggest such a theory to—to intelligent men? We, who have proven the utter untouchability of thought! Why, I—"

"Sit down, my dear sir," Dunn suggested coolly. "Proof of my assertions will shortly be forthcoming. In the meantime, let me explain further. Any wave in ether—or at any rate in the medium we call 'ether' for want of a better name—is basically composed of electrons and atoms. All of them are invisible, but those whose aggregates build up into sight formation we call 'visible matter-things;' those whose ultimate vibration remains beyond visual perception we call 'mental.' But the fact remains that both states have basic atoms and, therefore, are capable of annihilation and release of energy. In the one, matter energy. In the other, thought energy."

"Since they are both basically electrical, how do you expect to get anything but electrical energy from either of them?" Maxwell asked.

"Because if I scooped a bucket in a pond I wouldn't expect it to come up full of soil," Dunn blandly answered.

At that there was a faint chuckle of amusement from the newspapermen, increasing as Maxwell stood glowering down on the savant.

"Meaning just what?" he demanded heavily.

"Meaning that matter atoms release the electrical essence of matter energy because they *are* matter atoms, and meaning that thought-energy atoms will release the essence of thought energy because they are thought atoms. The mental atoms and their waves create all our powers of perception—they bridge that mystic gap in the brain that lies between seeing a thing and interpreting its nature. They are at the basis of all conception, ideation, creation and imagination. And where necessary, the brain control of these waves can make mental conception become a physical realization."

Maxwell cried, "Such balderdash! You expect us to believe *that?*"

"I'll show you," Dunn said, turning aside. He walked across to his aluminum chair and sat in it. Operating the switches on the arms, he set the bladed rotor twirling ever his head.

"This," he said quietly, "is a mental wave pick-up, so designed that the invisible play of waves from my brain—the tiny electrical impulses—are passed to it and transferred as potential to the two spheres you see up there. Normally, those spheres are used for normal energy, which you will see later. This is merely a side line to the main experiment to prove my point." He turned and raised his thin hand. "O.K., Allan!" he cried.

Allan nodded and gave the signal to the engineers. The various machines, operating only on 75% of the power used for normal atomic disruption, began to hum softly. The rotor span with swift, easy revolutions. In silence the audience watched, studying Dunn's lined face as he sat concentrating for nearly seven minutes. Then he gave the halt signal and rose to his feet.

"Now, gentlemen," he said, "the essence of the thought waves radiated by me is stored as potential in those spheres. In the vacuum tube globe, as you can see for yourselves through the inspection plate, is a mass of nerve tissue representing the materials found in a human brain. Once the master switch is thrown here the force of those potential mental waves of mine will strike on that inert substance and pattern it instantly into the thing I have mentally pictured—a human brain of considerable size. Is that clear?"

Maxwell folded his arms obstinately; "Well, what are we waiting for?" he asked shortly. "Let's see your conjuring trick."

With a chuckle Dunn turned aside. "What's the reading, Allan?"

"Potential 50,000 volts mental energy," Allan crisped back, scanning his meters.

"Do not confuse thought energy with normal-energy readings, my friends." Dunn smiled, looking round. "50,000 volts of mental energy is quite high, believe me! Now, let us see—"

He turned swiftly toward the master switches and clamped his hand down on the principal one. Dryly he said, "Watch the target chamber of the tube, Maxwell. You're sure you can see it clearly?"

"Go right ahead," the irritated psychist growled, and sat with beard projecting and face elevated in the air.

A silence fell on the laboratory; every eye directed itself to the vacuum tube's inspection chamber. The generators of the strange contrivance hummed with sudden vigor. In one clean movement Dunn slammed in the master switch.

Immediately the energy flared brilliantly from positive and negative spheres, burst in a crackling, crisping roar in the target chamber. For a fraction of a second the daylighted laboratory was bathed in a brilliance comparable only with the sudden ignition of large quantities of magnesium—then the disturbance died away and the engines stopped their droning.

Petrified, the spectators stared at the flawless brain clearly visible in the transparent globe, reposing exactly in the same spot as those former synthetic tissue elements. Maxwell sank back in his chair for a moment with a gasp, his lips tight behind his beard. He ignored the excited conversation of the assembled scientists, the chattering of the newspapermen. For the life of him he could not take his gaze off that thing of gray. The voice of Dunn seemed.to reach him from a great distance.

"Well, my dear Maxwell, are you satisfied?"

He jerked himself into action. His cold eyes looked away from the brain to the savant. "I don't believe it!" he stated flatly. "All you've done is perform some damned clever conjuring trick! It just can't be done!"

Dunn was not annoyed, he merely shrugged. "You'd better examine it for yourself. Allan will show you how to enter the target chamber from the sphere. But take care you don't touch that brain. It's alive."

That was the last straw for Maxwell. He shot to his feet. "Alive!" he yelled.

"Certainly. Matter life is entirely at the dictates of mental waves. I willed the power of life into the energy that begot that brain, just as I fashioned it with my own concentration. Life is not a matter of hearts, lungs and blood. Life is an accidental arrangement of chemicals—a fortuitous concourse of atoms, as the experts call it. That atomic arrangement of life can quite easily be forced into being, be patterned, by mental waves. Don't forget the miracles of old. Don't forget how the belief in illness, particularly in the case of a hypochondriac, can produce the identical physical results. There you have a small example admitted in every medical realm."

Maxwell hesitated on something, then he tugged his beard fiercely. "Either way, I intend to examine that—that brain!" he announced curtly.

Dunn bowed pleasantly and signaled Allan. The young man was as curious as the elderly psychist as he guided up the ladder into the sphere. Together they stood looking in silence on that palpitating thing of gray in the matrixed globe of the target chamber. Beyond question it *was* a brain, definitely human in shape but far beyond average size. Even as they stood beside it they could feel a certain aura of compelling mental force radiating from it.

Msxwell turned away at last, his face astounded. Behind him the other scientists and eager reporters retreated, talking excitedly. Once down on the laboratory floor again the psychist regarded Dunn steadily for a moment, then with a sudden impulse held out his hand.

"I'm afraid I've been something of an old-fashioned fool, Dunn," he said very quietly. "I know a brain when I see one, and the only way that one could ever get into that globe is by the method you used. But man alive!" he went on incredulously, "think of the possibilities! To create whatever you choose at will and—"

"Ah, but that isn't exactly the idea." Dunn smiled. "The real demonstration has yet to come."

"So."

"I intend to annihilate that brain with 14,000,000 volts of energy, destroy the very mental atoms of its composition and release the intra-atomic energy of thought."

"But why? If you can create these things—"

"To create such things is but to scratch the surface of a vast unlocked core of mental power. The brain there is material, of course, but within it—even as inside our brains—repose myriad of mental atoms, the transparent matter electrons, of which I told you. My electricity here will store up a potential of 7,000,000 positive and 7,000,000 negative in either sphere. Before it leaves the generators it will pass through special transformers which will alter its frequency to that of the mentality atoms."

"And the release of this thought energy goes where?" Maxwell asked.

"You noticed that the brain lay within a globe and that the globe was fitted with four concave reflectors with their foci directed on the brain's center?"

"Yes, but what—"

"That globe is probably the most unbreakable, yet transparent, in existence. It is made of *tyuminite,* an extract of a rare Antarctica mineral deposit. It is built in two interlocking hemispheres, both of which took twelve years each to grind and shape. The entire globe will withstand the force of 14,000,000 volts energy because it allows free passage of force between the molecules of its construction. But whatever is within it will be utterly shattered and release itself in energy—in this case the brain's thought energy."

"You mean that the thought energy will be released and be unable to escape the globe, but that the brain shell will be left behind, devoid of mentality?" questioned Crawford.

"Just that; but the brain shell will disappear because the only thing holding it in consciousness is itself—its knowledge of *being.* It is storing thoughts and impressions right now like any ordinary brain. Afterward, the globe will be removed and by means of the wired terminals and inner contacts passing through it, it will be enabled to release its thought energy little by little into machines specially designed to absorb it. I'll show you those later. Now let us begin. It will take an hour to store our potential energy, so while that is taking place you must have some refreshment."

Dunn turned aside and signaled Allan. Immediately the generators commenced their whining. Within the immense spheres the machines began their gradual building up of potential energy—

III.

An hour later Allan announced that the potential reading for each sphere was 7,000,000 volts. It was the signal for the scientists and newspapermen to return to the laboratory and resume their seats.

The change in the manner of Maxwell was plainly noticeable. From being sour-faced and critical he had become almost eager. But his face was concerned as he asked, "Are you sure your tube will stand such a terrific blast as 14,000,000 volts?"

Dunn turned from the switchboards with a shrug. "According to all my tests it should certainly do so. If not—well, another tube will be built, that's all. Science never acknowledges defeat."

He grasped the main switch and glanced at Allan.

"All set, dad. Both spheres identically charged."

Dunn hesitated for a moment, glanced at the silent but living brain high up in the tube target chamber, then jammed in the master switch.

Immediately the tearing, battering fury of man-made thunder and lightning burst free in the great tube. Its enormous length became a brilliant, blinding furnace of raging varicolored light. Crackling din deafened every ear; an enormous surge of static energy sent a crimping sensation through the hair of everybody present.

Then above the din Allan gave a hoarse shout. "Dad! The tube's cracking! Look—"

The professor didn't answer. He was standing gripping his switch fiercely, staring with unbelieving eyes. Beyond question the tube *was* breaking. A slow fissure had appeared along its length from the center, warping swiftly with the seconds from that main core of unguessable energy impacts—

"Run for it!" Allan cried desperately, racing toward his father.

But he was too late. At that identical moment the enormous tube shattered outward in a spraying fury of glass shards. The din of a terrific explosion gushed through the laboratory, hurled back newspapermen and scientists in a scorched, blinded jam, ears deafened by the hellish noise.

Walls quaked under the force; instruments collapsed. Free energy hurled itself in momentary writhing streamers on every possible contact with earth. Something ground and rended mightily.

Then came silence—a tense, uncanny silence, all the more potent by reason of the din that had preceded it.

Allan stirred weakly from the floor and pushed away a metal strut that had fallen across him. His hand found a freely bleeding cut on his cheek. Scrambling to his feet, he stared dully around him. On every side was crumbled wreckage. Only the walls of the laboratory were left standing; the windows were cracked to pieces. The huge vacuum tube was utterly shattered; the energy spheres were slued at a drunken angle, torn wires draping around them.

His gaze went swiftly over the struggling scientists and newspapermen as they got painfully to their feet, some of them bleeding, others hardly scratched. Maxwell rose up with his gray hair hanging absurdly down his face, his collar torn from its stud. So much Allan grasped, then he caught sight of his father lying prone on the floor, half covered by a fallen girder support from the tube.

Long before he reached him Allan instinctively knew he was dead. He knelt beside him—involuntary tears in his eyes—tugging uselessly at the girder. The dead face of the scientist was half smiling; one thin hand clenched a broken piece of switch. Death must have been instantaneous. The weight of the girder had crushed the life out of him.

The rest was a blur to Allan. Maxwell, aided by Van Linman and Crawford, worked desperately with the newspapermen to raise the girder. It took ten of them to do it. The body beneath was hopelessly crushed.

Maxwell shook his head bitterly. "He ought never to have used such power!"

"But what caused it?" Allan shouted hoarsely, abruptly coming to himself. "Why did such a thing have to happen on the very verge of success? Why did—"

"It was the terrific power, boy, nothing else," Maxwell muttered. "I half expected it—" He turned and looked upward. The assembly did likewise.

"The brain's gone, anyhow," muttered Van Linman. "It must have been annihilated. Wonder if the mental atoms were able to release their thought energy?"

"I no longer care one way or the other," Allan said hollowly. "The whole experiment's a failure. It's brought nothing but disaster and the death of my father." He tried to get a hold on himself. "Give me a hand to carry him into the house, will you?"

Nobody spoke, but with a certain reverence the disheveled, blood-stained men moved forward to obey his behest.

* * * *

The newspapers carried the fullest details of the explosion at the laboratory, lauded Professor Dunn's achievements up to the skies, and closed with the regret that he had died and taken his profound knowledge with him. For Allan, though he knew the outline, would need to still study for years before he could possibly rediscover from his father's notes the secret of matter creation from thought.

Not that he had the inclination in any case. The accident that had killed the old man and brought an abrupt end to his magnificent researches had made Allan embittered and disinclined to pursue that particular field any further.

Instead, he devoted his time to normal physics and left mental mechanics severely alone—until one day, to his great surprise, he had a visit from Dr. Maxwell. The psychist's face was very serious; only something of grave import could possibly have brought him 3,000 miles from a busy professional life to the scene of that earlier disaster.

Somewhat puzzled, Allan accompanied him into the house. Over his glass of refreshment Maxwell regarded him seriously.

"Allan, I'm here as a direct result of chance observations I have made over in California, also because of a rather alarming theory I have in mind. In brief, in various parts of the country, but in California in particular, certain vital plants of the lower species have ceased growing—ceased growing *now,* at the most fruitful time of the year! And what is more, they are disappearing!"

Allan managed to state a polite "Really?" He gazed at the lean-faced scientist in vague bewilderment.

"That seems a small thing, doesn't it?" Maxwell went on, draining his glass. "On the contrary, though, I believe it to be the most significant thing that ever happened! Plants, we admit, have a certain power of instinctive thought, have they not?" Allan nodded slowly, frowning.

Maxwell went on, "They also represent the least intelligent form of life. After them come the more intelligent germ life— the amoeba, the animalcule, and so forth; after that, the animals; after that again, man—the highest state. Now suppose some power, starting at the bottom of the intellectual scale, were annihilating the power of thought completely? Plants would cease to grow at first, would they not, and then disappear, for they would have no power of conception to hold them in being?"

Allan looked startled. "I suppose that's right, but— Look here, doctor, what on earth are you getting at?"

Maxwell leaned forward earnestly. "Just to the fact that I think your father's experiment with mental atoms *was* a success of the most disastrous kind that ever came to our knowledge! He converted me into a firm believer of his magnificent scientific ability—so much so that since the accident I have thought of little else but that effort to release intra-atomic thought energy. Suppose, though, instead of just shattering the atoms, he utterly blasted thought energy itself back into the state from which it originally evolved? That, in the case of the total destruction of an atom of *matter* and its energy, would mean the slow collapse of the known universe. If it can happen to a matter atom, then, as science has fully proved, there is nothing to stop it happening to a mental atom. You see my point?"

Allan sank down rather weakly into a chair, trying to grapple with the psychist's cold logic.

"But how can such a thing have happened? My father had every detail at his fingertips—"

"I'm not saying he hadn't, but the best of us can err, especially in so complicated a matter as thought. The dividing line between releasing intra-atomic energy and forcing it back— telescoping its evolution to a primal state—is amazingly slight, as our own scientists well know. Some fortune has always saved us so far from utterly annihilating a piece of *matter* into its primal state. But it's beginning to look as though no such fortune favored your father's experiment. He clearly stated, and there is much to substantiate him now, that matter and mind are evolved products of the same thing at different vibrational rates. Both states have progressed uniformly from one point, and that point was No Thing. Do you understand?"

"I know nothing against it," Allan confessed.

Maxwell considered briefly. "Well, I've worked out a theory, and my only hope is that it's wrong! If your father created primal thought energy—an energy existing at the time of our universe being born—it will mean a gigantic shifting, a veritable de-evolution through the whole structure of intelligence itself. And since matter cannot exist without intelligence, it means that that will be destroyed, too!"

Allan's face blanched. "But that cannot be!" he cried hoarsely. "Such a thing just couldn't happen!"

"Unfortunately, it could," Maxwell said gravely. "That energy was not trapped as was intended. It was allowed to go free, to seep out. Inside that brain was the energy of incalculable numbers of mental atoms. Millions of years of mental evolution must have instantly telescoped into primal energy, such as could only have existed in the beginning. It will destroy the very structure of mentality, until finally—well, we don't know what will take place. Obviously, the least intelligent things will go first. The higher states will come afterward as the energy finds a more uniform level and re-patterns everything to its original formula. That original formula is literally nothing—the substance of emptiness, if I may use the phrase—the state that must have existed before our primal atom exploded and evolved into mind and matter."

"Good Lord!" Allan breathed weakly, staring before him. "And—and there's no telling where these things may happen! The energy will have spread out, impacted with mental waves both great and small. You think that those disappearing plants are the first signs?"

Maxwell brooded. "What else? There is no other possible explanation. What we've got to do is to go through your father's notes, examine the situation in every aspect, and see if there is not some possible way of averting this disaster. He of all people could probably have found a negative result—"

His face became suddenly earnest. "Listen, Allan! I'm willing to sacrifice all my time and energy to solving the problem. I've made arrangements for a prolonged absence from Los Angeles. We've just got to try and find a way to avert this disaster!"

"Dad's notes are all in the library," Allan said, a little dazedly, as he got to his feet. "Come along with me."

Just as Maxwell had feared, however—and Allan too, though he had not openly admitted the fact—the dead professor's notes proved too complicated to follow at short notice. It would demand the work of years to follow all his theories. Even if that could be accomplished, there was no telling how much longer it would take after that to produce a negative result and circumvent the grim thing that had happened. There simply was not time.

The fact became evident to the two after three days and nights of continuous analysis of sheet after sheet of abstruse formulae. At the end of the time, sleepless and exhausted, they were forced to the realization that they were no nearer than when they had started.

Allan looked at the psychist's lean face anxiously. "Supposing—supposing you are right?" he said dully. "How long have we before we're overtaken?"

Maxwell slowly shook his head. "How can I say? It is not in my power to outline the activity of a primal energy. It may do anything! It may achieve some strange level of its own and leave us free. But on the other hand—and the most likely occurrence—it will force things back to an original state. It will undo the work of the accident that started the universe. Maybe only weeks—maybe centuries. We cannot tell."

He fell silent and they stood looking helplessly at each other, surrounded by their piles of useless data.

IV.

Mankind in general was not immediately aware of anything unusual interfering with its daily progress. Most of the vital news had been suppressed by Maxwell himself. But here and there certain famous dailies asked trenchant questions. They demanded to know, for instance, what was happening to plants and orchards in various parts of the country.

Not only in the United States, but all over the world there were distinct signs of plant failure, followed immediately afterward by a complete disappearance. At the start such stories were put down to over-imaginative reporters or to the visions of a drunk. But when a 300-year-old beech tree vanished overnight from the garden of a famous senator, leaving pure undisturbed earth behind it, the matter took a serious turn. The senator was famous. He could not possibly have been drunk. Science was called upon to explain.

There was no success in this direction. Maxwell and Allan Dunn, the only two who could give the truth, purposely refused to do so. It would only mean the precipitation of a panic. But they forgot that perhaps one of the reporters attending the earlier experiment might form a theory. Blake, of the *Times,* actually did so and ran a feature article on the subject, clinging very closely to Maxwell's own theories, though by no means as technical.

Cold logic was his keynote. Did science realize, he asked, that the slow disappearance of plant life—whether explainable or not—would mean the death of mankind not only from starvation, but from the lack of anything to absorb the continuous flow of carbon dioxide being perpetually breathed into the atmosphere? Since it was an inevitable fact that any living organism must die in its own waste, it was clear that humanity would start to die once the proportion of organic creatures overbalanced those of the inorganic.

This observation sent a stir through the scientists. It began to dawn on them with vivid clearness that something unknown *was in* their very midst. The only thing to do was to erect machinery at top speed for the absorption of carbon dioxide. It demanded money—an enormous supply of it—but the gathering threat of vanishing vegetation the world over forced governments into lending their aid. Accordingly, there sprouted in all directions gigantic editions of the carbon-dioxide machinery used aboard stratosphere planes and deep-sea bathyspheres. Mankind breathed more freely in consequence, blissfully confident that the trouble would soon blow over.

But it didn't. In mutual despair, Maxwell and Allan watched the slow but inevitable vanishing of whole continents of grass and trees. Central Africa, in the space of a month, became as bare as the Arabian Desert. The foliage of the British Isles, pride of the Britons, melted like mist before a hot sun. Without sound, without apparent movement, grass and trees were scalped clean from the earth; whole rivers of emptiness crawled night and day down the lofty timber-forested hills of Canada. The mystic disease left nothing behind it—not a single blade of grass, not a single root that could ever sprout again.

The finger of grim, mysterious tragedy stirred up the melting pot of frantic humans and sent them scurrying to all quarters of the earth, full of threats, demands and suggestions. Timbermen, lumberjacks, scientists, farmers and agriculturists scattered to the four quarters of the vegetation-disrobing world to study and ponder a wholly inexplicable problem.

In time the riddle became classified; very aptly, as 'Racing Baldness' But there was nobody on earth that could keep up with it. Expert horticulturists, champion flower growers and botanists met in solemn conclave and discussed learnedly all the flower diseases they'd ever encountered or heard of. Such things as dry rot, double striping, wet streak and root warp filled the air of their meeting chambers. But the fact remained that when they had finished and passed several resolutions, their champion specimens—either vegetable or flower—had disappeared forever from their sight and knowledge.

The certain maddening inevitability of disappearing green stuff the world over completely upset man's delicately balanced emotions. An immense wave of panic and despair ruthlessly gripped every country; the foundations of everyday commerce were literally being cut away. Fortunes tottered and vanished overnight. Stocks and shares, wheat and corn markets became the rampage grounds for frantic, penniless investors. Ellerman K. Hicks, the corn cob king, shot himself in full view of thousands of harassed associates. With the action he started a world-wide epidemic of suicides.

Magnates whose fortunes relied basically on the world's staple food supplies eliminated themselves one after the other. Those of their staff who were left behind tried vainly to salve something from the wreckage. The Racing Baldness just went on, grew and grew, never disturbing anything, simply lifting away green stuff as though it were dissolving steam.

* * * *

In four months the African and South American jungles had gone; in five, the immense redwood and sequoia forests of California had followed them; in eight months practically every country was empty of green. Grass, desert scrub, trees, vines, even sea kelp and algae had all disappeared. For the first time in history the Sargasso Sea became easily navigable.

In a year there was a bald world. Throughout that entire year Maxwell and Allan had toiled mightily on the dead professor's notes, working every possible hour, sleeping and eating only when sheer necessity compelled it, aided now in their Herculean struggles by the best scientific minds the world had ever produced—but still the same unsurmountable riddles rose up.

Professor Dunn had been a phenomenon among men. He had devoted a supreme brain to one sole subject, mastered it so perfectly that other men, trained in other directions, could not immediately correlate the profundity of his conceptions. Time, too, was fast catching up. Soon there would not be a chance. The world was already in chaos, and that only marked the beginning.

By the time total baldness had arrived, when not a single blade of grass was anywhere to be found, the news burst from various quarters that animalcule life was vanishing from ponds, lakes and rivers—snuffing out as mysteriously as the plants had done. Two drops of water extracted from a notably life-infested lake in Central America revealed the fact that not a trace of bacterial or microbial life was within it. The water had a purity beyond all belief.

Added to this fresh riddle was the increasing problem of caring for cattle. The supply of synthetic, nitrogenous materials could not last indefinitely. Besides, there were distinct evidences that these materials were in an unstable state, bordering on collapse and ultimate disappearance. When that happened, humanity would be in the grip of a famine already manifesting itself in outlying districts beyond the major cities.

Back in New York, Maxwell, Allan and the scientists considered the new problem of vanishing little life.

"It's working out just as I predicted," Maxwell said drearily. "The escaped mental energy is assimilating the least intelligent things in order of progression. First the plants went; then there occurred what we might call a mutational process; it moved up to the absorption of the next highest mental state and is resolving it back into a primal state. That embraces the whole range of little things—microbes, amoebae, bacteria, the living mites inside our own blood streams—everything! It is the total end of all humanity, of the world—maybe of the universe!"

How true his statement was became vividly revealed in the speeding weeks. Mankind, milling helplessly and uselessly to all quarters of the world, learned of the slow evaporation of little life from earth's face. Then the first stages of the disaster struck home to them, personally, as their own blood streams and lymph were affected. The effect did not entirely kill them, but produced a violent form of pernicious anemia—left them scraggy, weary, cadaverous of face, bloodless of skin. Utter blight had drained health forever from every men, woman and child on the earth.

Animals were likewise. Cattle began to die off at lightning speed. But presently the 'disappearing' epidemic caught up with them and eradicated them completely before they had a chance to die.

Confused and bewildered, sick and weary in mind and body, humans tried to grasp what it was all about, and in the main they failed. The weakest began to die off from starvation and anemia. Here and there a few managed to keep going, but for all that humanity's numbers were sliced to three quarters, and then a half, as the depressing months sped onward.

Maxwell, Allan and the scientists scarcely looked human any longer. They were gaunt-faced, white-skinned, creases of exhaustion and strain carved deep into their faces. Their clothes were dirty, their hair unshorn and flowing. Maxwell's beard straggled half down his chest.

"There's nothing now can save us," was his hopeless pronouncement when they came to review the situation. "Little life and greenery have gone. Now the mutation—if we can call it such—embraces cattle. Next it will be us. The process is moving much faster than at the commencement. Everything—*everything*—is resolving back to primal nothingness. The carbon-dioxide machines are still functioning, I understand, but they can't last much longer. Men and women are dying at their posts from sheer starvation and illness—"

"And so shall this unsubstantial pageant fade and leave not a wrack behind," Allan murmured, slumped in his chair with his eyes half-closed. "I guess Goldsmith was a darn sight nearer the truth than he ever reckoned when he made that statement."

None of the others answered him. Words were no longer worth using; they meant nothing. The free release of primal thought energy had laid the foundations of entire universal collapse.

The ever-advancing tide of disappearance increased tenfold as it progressed. It leaped from the annihilation of little things and animals to embrace human beings in an incredibly swift pace of time.

The majority of people whom it first attacked were hardly aware of the fact. They were close to death anyway. Here and there a few of the hardier spirits were trailing uselessly into barren green-bare lands, unable to believe that Earth's mantle had gone and could never return. Then, soundlessly—out of the birdless, windless air—that unknown impalpable power swept in and engulfed them.

Nor was it long before it crept up on New York and evaporated the once teeming populace from that now stagnant metropolis. It eradicated humanity from the streets, the slums, the harbors, the pestilential spots—the million and one odd corners still left untouched even by the sweeping brush of the 21st century. It lifted the rich and the poor, man and woman and child, and left not a trace behind.

It silently caught up with the drowsing, weary scientists in Dunn's laboratory and misted them to each other's gaze before they could utter a word or raise a finger. But it was not, as Allan rapidly discovered, an entire oblivion. Evidently that atavism to a primal state had still a long way to go so far as the individual consciousness was concerned.

Certainly he was devoid of body, almost before he knew it—cut off from all human associations, lost forever to Maxwell and the other scientists, to all he had ever known or loved. But he was still able to penetrate the veil with the forces of his slowly retreating mentality, able to behold those last hours of earth as, disembodied, dissociated from what other minds there might be around him, he moved hither and thither at the mercy of unknown ethereal shiftings and patternings, following that incredible de-evolution back into the very womb of creation.

He became the impartial witness of astounding things— things that occasioned no emotions, for his body was no longer present to agitate or electrify his nerves. With every second he could feel his comprehension slipping—slipping—slipping, as mentality was more and more resolved into one great common oneness.

Empty New York was before him. Momentarily it was the New York of 2069 he had always known, with its rearing spires and towers of evenly splashed windows, hiding behind them offices and apartments of a race now forever lifted from the world. Beyond the major spires squatted the heavier bulks of many hotels—darkly unlighted from within—catching the glimmer of a sinking western sun on their summits.

The canyons of streets, the broad tree-empty squares, the silent upjutting fountain jets were the deserted, flawless patchwork of a huge metropolis at the end of a life well and truly lived—a mass of erections to the memory of humanity poised almost on the edge of the harbor. There were motionless ships, anchored and abandoned, some with flags still flapping with a forlorn dreariness in the soft western wind. Soundlessly the oily waters slapped beneath their bows.

A toy city crouched on Manhattan Island—that was how it looked. Then, as the mind of Allan Dunn shifted toward it by an unknown, sub-ethereal current, he saw the first evidences of a change—the first collapse occasioned by the final extinction of every form of little life that had ever existed—a vast mutation of destruction finally and absolutely completed.

Momentarily it was born to him that there was a reason—beside that of the little things, the bacteria and the myriad animalcules—making up the very solidity of the ground itself. The mind of man had built New York, had built every known habitation on the Earth. But it only existed so long as man held it in mind. Now, with the rapid digression of multimillions of minds into a backward state, that conception was fading with the rapidity of a dream.

The mind of Allan Dunn perceived, dispassionately, all-inclusive. He saw the mighty towers fade or slide down into each other like creations of warm wax. Apparently solid masonry and stone merged and sluiced into each other with soundless unity. The windows became part of the surrounding stone and the stone became a crawling plasma that slumped down into a uniform, consistent level, filling streets that were only transiently present.

Buildings, streets and squares slipped into one fading conglomeration of unknown substance—flowed outward to the silent sea and yet vanished long before reaching it. Vaporized like fog and leaving behind a virgin purity of undisturbed soil, the harbor waters writhed strangely and the ships disappeared. The wafers flowed gently inward over wooden pillars that also slid into the indefinable consistency of the unknowable and likewise ceased to be.

Far away the sun touched the calm western horizon.

Maybe the disappearance of the city took a few minutes, or it might have been centuries. The mind of Allan Dunn, now so far retrograded, had almost lost cognizance of time. He only knew that man's withdrawn conception had also withdrawn the city of his creation, even as an awakening destroys the seemingly solid fabric of a dream. And since light, atmosphere and earth itself are but figments, he beheld, also, their slow dissolution.

He seemed to recede in space as he beheld it, or else it was the earth itself which shrank. He could not be sure—

V.

Water and land flowed toward a certain inevitable union. The land submerged; the mountains and hills leveled themselves to join the plains; the plains slipped below the sliding, inexorable tides. Every upraised level of land, every sign of a gorge or chasm ceased to be and sank smoothly to flatness. The waters rolled on. But they, too, eddied strangely and began to become transparent, shuddered and began to melt in fast-spreading patches of nothingness. Atmosphere, water, the very form and shape of earth were disappearing into a soundless eternity of void.

Within seeming moments earth had gone. The void remained, star-ridden, endless, sunless—for the sun, too, had gone with the earth. There was no moon, nor anything that had ever been visible from earth. Mars, Venus, Mercury—the giant outer planets—had snuffed out and left the endless dark. Constellations shifted and winked, became formations that had existed at some preceding point of time.

The mind of Allan Dunn drifted, onward and ever backward, toward the remote primary of all things. With that drifting, he realized the vague truth that he had been born before—that earth had not been his only world of existence. He had lived and breathed and struggled on other worlds, in other states in other bodies, in other times—frontiers of the utterly forgotten were laid bare to him as he devolved back to the state whence he had come.

The star-lighted eternity gave place at intervals to the fleeting, phantom concepts of other worlds, populated by beings with whom he felt a certain kinship, whose secrets he had mastered, whose science was something incredible in its superlative efficiency. Then the knowledge had gone; he fitted miraculously into a world as fair as earth had been. He loved and died there—a being of no importance, but fitted none the less with sensations, hopes and ideals.

That, too, went—gave way to the void again, left him with the fading conviction that mind and matter, while undoubtedly differently evolved products of the same thing, could spread themselves over a variety of ramifications, just as matter can divide itself in a lowly form and produce millions from one cell. How otherwise, in this backward transit, could he account for the fact that parts of his complete mind had been scattered promiscuously throughout the universe—that in some places he had been transcendentally clever, in others as non-intelligent as an imbecile?

Now, on the retreating trail, he embraced all these mental forms, drew together the threads of his one unity, even as a backwardly growing plant might encompass the myriad grown plants spawned from its original seed—each of them apparently living an independent existence at the same instant of time.

Then the comprehension was gone. He could no longer conceive its potent meaning.

His mind swept back over formless corridors of untold epochs and millenia of time—encompassing the shadowy, the vital, the meaningless, the incredible. Ghosts of a myriad strange lives and minds flowed together as one mental unit and passed through his receding mind without meaning. Ephemeral glimpses of worlds of vapor, cold, heat and pure energy passed him by and meant nothing.

The cosmos shifted again. He was a gyrating, backwardly hurtling point in a contracting universe. He slipped over a thousand million years into backwardness as though it were but an instant. Time, speed, distance and dimensions had ceased to register. He no longer knew methods of comparison, only knew the things that were. He snatched at and lost the flashing, practical evidences of proof that might have helped him.

Helplessly dissociated, yet with the dim conviction of drawing into a contracted oneness with other widespread arms of his mind, he contracted further and further toward the unknown beginning of time. Earth? New York? They were things that had no meaning, that had never been, that never would be, except as remote postulations of an expanding thought. He was contracting toward the beginning, not expanding toward finality, therefore such postulations were without shape or meaning.

Still the variety of lives slipped past his consciousness. He lived inside the stars, trod their incredibly heavy black surfaces, looked out from unknown outposts upon glassy seas that mirrored those same stars with a certain irresistible meaning. He moved through the interstices of solid matter; he existed in a deep ocean under inconceivable pressures.

Abruptly he was in three places at once, conscious of three distinct entities moving uniformly along one time track. The conception shifted—he was four-dimensional, extending into unknown space wherein no matter was closed.

Then again the aloneness, the growing weariness, the dreary emptiness of isolated movement. His conceptions weakened. He rose less high in the scale of intelligence. He remained in a rut of small conceiving that encompassed only the lowly intellect of an animal. The same incredible variety was there. He was an animal in every shape and possibility, sometimes a mere postulation along a line that never reached finality, at others a slowly moving squid in the deeps of an ocean, or a clumsy-footed beast on an unknown plain, caring for nothing save his immediate needs.

Sometimes he was hunted; at others he was the hunter. He lived and died. He died and lived—in a different species. He had his abode high up on a storm-bound cliff; he fought for his mate against a sky line that sprouted trees of no conceivable shape or meaning—figments, flashes, snapshots, momentary glimpses out of the vast evolution of mind and matter from its primal state.

Then suddenly he was fighting for his life in the blood stream of an unknown animal. He knew only life and death and food—a swift parasitical existence that faded as quickly into a stationary form wherein he had branches and drooped with forlorn abandon on the shore of a steaming ocean.

The shuttling visions faded. He was back in an infinity that was sparse with stars—stars that winked and trembled and faded one by one. Around him, about him on every hand he could feel a gathering oppression—mental oppression, enormous and crushing, the forcing together of a myriad mental states into their primal formation.

Distant hazy islands of light came scudding soundlessly toward him—the enormous masses of cosmic energy that had been hurled apart at the birth of the universe, at the rupture of the primordial atom of space, time, matter and mind.

The pull of opposing radiations, the reason for cosmic birth, was momentarily strong upon him, outweighed only by that ghastly sense of ever-increasing mental pressure—a gigantic squeezing, the stresses and strains of a primordial atom returning to its primal state.

The distant nebula swept incredibly nearer, inward—inward—ever inward. The stars winked in their solitary positions and were not. Infinity was swallowing up in a soundless dark. Faster moved the nebulas, crushing inward—

The strain was beyond endurance. Twin radiations fused across each other, in reverse, produced an unimaginable impact out of which had been all that was—mind and matter, matter and mind.

But the conscious mind of Allan Dunn knew it not. His mind, every mind included in his own, had flowed together into the one primal state, literally been undisrupted and hurled over the barrier that had brought it into being. Beyond that state there lay nothing—only the formless and the dark, an emptiness that was devoid of radiation, of ether, of matter, of intelligence; a fixed and eternal unity of pure space in which no thing was present, in which no thing would ever be present, except the dark—the everlasting dark—

ABOUT THE AUTHOR

British writer **JOHN RUSSELL FEARN** was born near Manchester, England, in 1908. As a child he devoured the science fiction of Wells and Verne, and was a voracious reader of the Boys' Story Papers. He was also fascinated by the cinema, and first broke into print in 1931 with a series of articles in *Film Weekly*.

He then quickly sold his first novel, *The Intelligence Gigantic*, to the American magazine, *Amazing Stories*. Over the next fifteen years, writing under several pseudonyms, Fearn became one of the most prolific contributors to all of the leading US science fiction pulps, including such legendary publications as *Astounding Stories, Startling Stories, Thrilling Wonder Stories*, and *Weird Tales*.

During the late 1940s he diversified into writing novels for the UK market, and also created his famous superwoman character, The Golden Amazon, for the prestigious Canadian magazine, the Toronto *Star Weekly*. In the early 1950s in the UK, his fifty-two novels as "Vargo Statten" were bestsellers, most notably his novelization of the film, *Creature from the Black Lagoon*.

Apart from science fiction, he had equal success with westerns, romances, and detective fiction, writing an amazing total of 180 novels—most of them in a period of just ten years—before his early death in 1960. His work has been translated into nine languages, and continues to be reprinted and read worldwide.

JOHN RUSSELL FEARN

THE ANJANI SERIES

The Gold of Akada: A Jungle Adventure Novel
Anjani the Mighty: A Lost Race Novel

THE BLACK MARIA SERIES

Black Maria, M.A.: A Classic Crime Novel
The Murdered Schoolgirl: A Classic Crime Novel
One Remained Seated: A Classic Crime Novel
Thy Arm Alone: A Classic Crime Novel
Death in Silhouette: A Classic Crime Novel

THE HERBERT THE DINOSAUR SERIES

A Thing of the Past
The Genial Dinosaur

OTHER BOOKS

1,000-Year Voyage: A Science Fiction Novel
Account Settled: A Science Fiction Mystery
Bury the Hatchet: A Crime Tale
A Case for Brutus Lloyd: A Science Fiction Mystery
The Crimson Rambler: A Crime Novel
Don't Touch Me: A Crime Novel
Dynasty of the Small: Classic Science Fiction Stories
The Empty Coffins: A Mystery of Horror
The Fourth Door: A Mystery Novel
From Afar: A Science Fiction Mystery
Fugitive of Time: A Classic Science Fiction Novel
The G-Bomb: A Science Fiction Novel
Here and Now: A Science Fiction Novel
Into the Unknown: A Science Fiction Tale

Last Conflict: Classic Science Fiction Stories
Legacy from Sirius: A Classic Science Fiction Novel
The Man from Hell: Classic Science Fiction Stories
The Man Who Was Not: A Crime Novel
Manton's World: A Classic Science Fiction Novel
Moon Magic: A Novel of Romance (as Elizabeth Rutland)
One Way Out: A Crime Novel (with Philip Harbottle)
Pattern of Murder: A Classic Crime Novel
Reflected Glory: A Dr. Castle Classic Crime Novel
*Robbery Without Violence: Two Science Fiction Crime
    Stories*
Rule of the Brains: Classic Science Fiction Stories
Shattering Glass: A Crime Novel
The Silvered Cage: A Scientific Murder Mystery
Slaves of Ijax: A Science Fiction Novel
Something from Mercury: Classic Science Fiction Stories
The Space Warp: A Science Fiction Novel
The Time Trap: A Science Fiction Novel
Valley of Pretenders: Classic Science Fiction Stories
Vision Sinister: A Scientific Detective Thriller
Voice of the Conqueror: A Classic Science Fiction Novel
What Happened to Hammond? A Scientific Mystery
Within That Room!: A Classic Crime Novel
World Without Chance: Classic Science Fiction Stories

www.ingramcontent.com/pod-product-compliance
Lightning Source LLC
Chambersburg PA
CBHW020141180626
46810CB00004B/1668